ONE EYE OPEN

ONE EYE OPEN

ALEX GRECIAN

Illustrated by Andrea Mutti

One Eye Open by Alex Grecian

Illustrations by Andrea Mutti
Cover design by Julie Metz Design
Interior design by Amy Sumerton

All inquiries should be addressed to:
    TKO Studios, LLC
    1325 Franklin Avenue
    Suite 545
    Garden City, NY 11530

TKO STUDIOS is a registered trademark

Visit our website at tkopresents.com

First Edition
ISBN: 978-1-952203-29-9

Printed in the United States of America

For Graham.

—Alex

For Enio Faini,
my beloved uncle.

—Andrea

PROLOGUE

CHARLOTTE JESSEN stood at the kitchen window and watched the sun rise for the last time.

When the coffee pot finished percolating, she poured two cups and set one on the counter for Tor, when he came in from the fields. *If* he came in from the fields. Lately he had been spending all his time out there, tending the crop of winter wheat.

Charlotte spooned sugar into his cup. As she put the canister back in the cupboard, she brushed her fingertips over the new box of rat poison, next to the sugar and the flour in their matching canisters. It would be easy to add a little to his coffee. Not only easy—it would be the right thing to do.

Just to slow him down a bit; just to give herself an edge.

But Charlotte couldn't bring herself to do it. She closed the cupboard and sat down at the kitchen table across from Tor's cooling cup.

She sipped her coffee and savored the moment, watching shadows move across the floor as the sun rose higher in the sky. Light slanted through the window and the yellow curtains she had sewn in their first year of marriage. After Tor hung them up, he'd put his arm around her and said, "When the sun comes through them, they'll match the color of your hair."

That had been forty-two years ago. She noticed how dingy and dated those curtains looked now and wondered why she had never thought to replace them.

Too busy, she thought. *There's never enough time.*

She finished her coffee and was rising from the table to pour a second cup when the door swung open. Tor stood on the stone threshold and stared in at her. He looked confused and maybe angry; it was hard for Charlotte to read his expressions anymore. He had stopped wearing clothes the previous Sunday and had rebelled when Charlotte tried to dress him in his dark suit for church. She had hung the suit in his closet and had known then that their time together was growing short.

He took a step into the kitchen. His feet and ankles were caked with mud, his shins spattered with a dark substance that Charlotte guessed was blood. Something rippled and bulged under his skin, and she backed away from him, shamed by her fear but unable to help herself.

"Tor?"

He looked at her, and she was heartbroken to see that there was no recognition in his eyes.

She was a stranger to him now.

"Sit," she said. "I made coffee."

She glanced at the cupboard where the box of rat poison sat, unopened. It was too late for poison. She had waited too long. Tor made a deep, guttural noise and moved toward her. She braced herself against the counter.

"It's not your fault," she said. "I hope you can understand. I wanted a little more time."

She felt the warm sun on the back of her neck and thought of her wedding day, and tried to smile at her husband as he threw the table against the wall. It dented the plaster and banged into the side of the refrigerator. Tor picked up one of the wooden chairs and broke it over his knee, slashing open his thigh. He did not bleed or even seem to notice. He tossed the pieces aside and rushed at Charlotte, his bare feet slapping on the clean kitchen floor, leaving a trail of dirt behind him.

"Goodbye, my love," Charlotte said. "Please forgive me."

THE DRIVER didn't get out to help. He popped the trunk and sat while Laura and Juniper Roux fetched their luggage. When they were done he gave them a limp wave through the side window, mumbled something in Danish, and drove away, leaving them alone at the gate of the little yellow farmhouse.

Laura looked up at it, picking out the window of her childhood bedroom, the ivy-covered trellis her first boyfriend had tried to climb, the sloped copper roof she had sat on while watching bonfires spread along the horizon every autumn.

It had been more than five years since she had last returned. More than five years since her father's funeral. Two days since her mother's.

"Do you remember this place?" she said.

"No," Juniper said. "It looks fake."

Laura looked again, trying to see it through her daughter's eyes. Compact and boxy, bright yellow with white trim. It did look plastic, modular—a child's playhouse with a picket fence and a covered porch. A gravel driveway circled the house, separating it from fields of wheat on one side and the stubby remains of harvested corn on the other. She could see the curved tin roof of the new barn and the tops of evergreen trees at the edge of the woods that grew wild behind the house.

She fished in the pocket of her jeans and found the key to

the front door. It had been messengered to her in Blue Valley and had now made its way back with them to its origin point, a journey of more than four thousand miles to an island off the coast of Denmark. Laura grabbed the handle of her roller bag and opened the gate.

"After you," she said.

Juniper sighed and led the way through, up the stone path to the porch.

"How long do we have to stay here?"

"I don't know," Laura said. "They already had the funeral, but I imagine there'll be some kind of memorial service. Who knows? Maybe we'll want to stay. Maybe we'll like it here."

Juniper rolled her eyes, and hoisted her luggage up the porch steps, waited while Laura fitted the key in the lock and opened the door. Laura had not told her daughter that they weren't going back. She hadn't found the words or the right time to say them. But their home in Blue Valley had been listed, and a realtor was handling the sale. Movers were already packing their things to ship to the farm. Laura had no plans to return.

"It smells like old people in here," Juniper said.

Laura sniffed. It smelled like her mother: wood polish and Cristalle and stale coffee. But there was an underlying sourness in the air, something stuffy and sad. It smelled like loneliness, and Laura felt a pang of guilt for staying away so long.

She remembered the house as being much larger, the front room big enough to hold a ball, the dark staircase winding endlessly up the north wall, the twin arches that led into the kitchen and her father's old study like the entrances to massive caves. Looking around now, she realized a small dinner party would crowd the place.

She went to a window and flung it open, inviting the October air inside. Behind her, Juniper bumped her suitcase up the stairs and Laura turned to watch as her daughter disappeared from sight, the wheels on her bag growling on the hardwood overhead.

"I get the big room," Juniper called down.

Laura shook her head and went to the bottom of the staircase.

"That's your grandmother's room," she said.

"So?" Juniper said, her voice faraway and muffled by thick walls and heavy air. "She's not using it, is she?"

Laura opened her mouth to reply, then thought better of it and crossed under the arch that led to the kitchen. Juniper had not been the same since the accident, and Laura wanted to spend some time alone with her daughter. She hoped time would make a difference.

The kitchen was small and tidy, with a round table in the corner. Three people might fit around it if they kept their elbows in close. Yellow curtains hung over the window, and copper pots hung from hooks over the fat round stove. The glass-fronted cabinets held neat rows of cups and plates, and a sturdy knife block held an assortment of blades.

Laura opened and closed drawers until she found her mother's utensils neatly organized in a plastic tray. She gathered up the steak knives from a slot and laid them on a dish towel along with a pair of kitchen shears, then emptied the knife block and rolled the towel up.

Laura threw the bolt on the back door and stepped outside onto the weathered stone patio. The house sat on a slight rise and she could see the neighboring fields of peas and corn and winter wheat that stretched in every direction to the horizon. Nothing had changed in the years since she left. She'd been so anxious to escape the farm community and attend university in America. She had packed a single bag and vowed never to return—but of course she had returned. For a funeral or two, for a school reunion, and for a holiday with Jacob to show him around the village where she was born.

Her feelings for the place had softened over time. *It's okay to leave and come back*, she thought. *The heart really does become fonder.*

She glanced at the corrugated tin barn and, beyond it, the tree line, dark and lush with vines growing through the underbrush, choking the old-growth spruce and the Douglas firs. If she walked around the side of the house, she knew she would be able to see past the crops to the outskirts of Godhavn.

She put a hand to her throat and sighed. Everything was so big and so small at the same time. She missed her husband, and she missed her daughter's smile. She hoped the fresh air, the community of Godhavn, and the surrounding farms would help draw Juniper out of her shell.

Laura found a depression in the dirt next to the house and wedged the towel in as far as she could, then covered it with a pile of dead leaves. She would have to do a better job of burying the knives before the leaves blew away, but it would do until morning. There was a big circle of charred earth in front of the barn. The ground there might be softer; it might be easier to dig a hole.

Returning to the kitchen, she paused at the threshold and looked down. Muddy footprints. Laura had not noticed them in the gloom, but the sun slanting through the open door delineated the curved shapes of two feet leading farther into the house. She followed the prints, but they faded as they crossed under the arch.

She used another dish towel to wipe the floor, then washed her hands at the sink and wheeled her suitcase to the stairs, pulling it behind her to the second story. There were three bedrooms, a tiny bathroom, and a walk-in linen closet with a chain lock on the outside of the door. Laura couldn't remember the chain being there before. She pulled it across its track and swung the door open, letting it dangle and rattle against the doorjamb. A moth fluttered out and brushed against her cheek. It settled on the wall across from her, two black spots on its gray wings like eyes, watching her.

Inside, the closet was cramped, the walls covered with floor-to-ceiling shelves stacked with towels and washcloths, sheets and pillowcases. The floor crackled under her feet and Laura realized she was standing on a thick blanket of powdery moth carcasses. Empty cocoons were webbed up in the corners where the shelves met the ceiling. She pulled a towel from the shelf in front of her and long strands of webbing followed it like gooey cheese. She dropped the towel and backed out of the closet, shutting the door and pulling the chain back along its track.

Her skin crawled with imagined insects. The moth still clung to the wall and she took a swipe at it. It flew away to the ceiling and spread its wings again, its black eye markings staring down at her.

Laura left her bag and walked down to her mother's old room at the end of the hall. The door was closed, and she knocked before entering. Juniper was lying on the queen-sized bed, squinting at her phone. She looked up at Laura and tossed her phone away. It bounced twice on the mattress and fell to the floor.

"No Wi-Fi here," Juniper said. "We're for real in the middle of nowhere."

"Maybe we can figure something out," Laura said. She picked up Juniper's phone and sat on the edge of the bed. "There must be some way to connect."

"How soon can we go home?"

Laura shrugged. "Let's see how it goes, okay?"

"What do people do around here?"

"We can ask when we go into town."

"But you used to live here, right? What did you do for fun?"

"I don't know. Bonfires and parties and hiking in the woods."

"I lied about being the outdoor type," Juniper said.

Laura smiled. Juniper was quoting the Lemonheads, one of Jacob's favorite bands. She was surprised to discover the reference didn't make her feel sad. She closed her eyes and took a breath that was redolent of Charlotte's perfume and powder. She was five years old again, with Charlotte's slender arms wrapped around her, protecting her. The room felt safe and solid, free from grief or loss or doubt.

"We have a little time before we're supposed to go into town," she said. "Help me find the washing machine. I want to get a load of towels started."

• 2 •

THEY LOCATED the washing machine behind a door in the kitchen. Juniper helped her mother carry towels and bedding downstairs. They shook out the husks of dead moths and picked off the webbing and poured more detergent into the machine than the directions indicated. Laura lugged a bucket of water back upstairs to the linen closet and they scrubbed the empty shelves. Juniper found a broom and dustpan and swept up the tiny carcasses from the floor while the moth on the ceiling watched her work. She turned the broom around and took a swipe at the moth, but only managed to smudge the white ceiling.

When the machine was done Laura hung the wet towels on a line in the yard, then they locked the front door and walked into town.

Godhavn was half a mile away, across a rutted dirt path that cut through fields of wheat. The sun was high in the west, and the blue sky was cloudless. They could smell the sea, but tall rows of wheat blocked their view of the water. Unseen insects sang to one another and a distant farmer waved at them from the high seat of his tractor. Juniper waved back, then stuck her hands in her pockets, embarrassed. She was wearing memory foam sandals and denim overalls, rolled up at the ankles. She meant the overalls to be vaguely ironic, some sort of commentary on the endless farmland around them. A grasshopper jumped across the path and Juniper recoiled. She felt itchy, as if something was burrowing under her skin.

There was a small scarecrow up ahead of them. It swayed from side to side in the light breeze, boneless, mimicking the top-heavy stalks of wheat on either side. When they drew closer to it, the scarecrow moved its head and looked directly at them. Laura realized it was a boy, maybe nine or ten years old, with straw-colored hair and pale skin. He smiled at them, then stepped to one side and disappeared into the rows. They watched both sides of the path and hurried a little faster. There had been something unnatural in the way the boy moved, and when he smiled at them the breeze had seemed colder.

After ten minutes the crops ended, and the path widened into a paved road that led into town. Once they had passed a handful of small outbuildings Godhavn seemed to sprout up around them, two- and three-story buildings crowded close together, all red and yellow and orange brick, peaked roofs with spires and weathervanes and ivy snaking along rain gutters. There was a narrow alley between two of the buildings, and they could see a small marina, boats bobbing up and down on the water, bumping against rubber tires lashed against the dock.

They peeked into the window of a cafe and saw two long tables surrounded by old women eating pastries. The next building housed a general store, cramped shelves piled with canned goods arranged in no discernible order.

"We'll need to stop on the way back and pick up some staples for the house," Laura said.

"Is there a pub here?" Juniper said. "What's the drinking age?"

Laura ignored her and they walked on until they reached an office wedged between a butcher shop and a bakery. A wooden sign hung from two hooks above the front door. KASPAR HENRIKSEN. No job title or description, just

a name. Everyone in town knew everyone else, and Kaspar Henriksen didn't need to advertise his occupation.

Laura pushed the door open without knocking and waved Juniper inside, where pale blue walls were scuffed along the baseboards, and mildew stains smothered the ceiling like lily pads. The hardwood floor was uneven, dark gaps between the planks forming a toothy grin. A massive, unmanned desk sat in the far corner. As they creaked across the front room, a door opened in the back wall and a mop of silver hair emerged, followed by a small, nervous man in a tweed suit several sizes too large for him. He rushed forward, leading with his head, and stuck out a pudgy hand. Laura took it, and he clasped her palm in both of his.

"*God eftermiddag,*" he said. "You must be Charlotte Jessen's daughter. Laura, yes? So good of you to make the trip."

Laura extricated her hand from his grip. "Thank you," she said.

He cleared his throat and glanced at the empty desk in the corner. "Apologies. Agnes is away again. Got to let the employees out every so often or they turn on you, yes?"

"I suppose so," Laura said.

"Oh," he said, "I forgot to introduce myself. I think perhaps you know that I am Kaspar Henriksen, your mother's lawyer. And I feel like I know you already, the way Charlotte talked about you. I wonder, do you still speak Danish?"

"I do, but it's been a long time. And Juniper doesn't, so we would prefer English, if you don't mind."

"And what is Juniper?"

"Juniper is my daughter," Laura said.

"Enchanté," Juniper said.

Laura frowned at her and Juniper raised her eyebrows and mouthed "what" silently.

"Daughter, you say," Henriksen said. He squinted again at Juniper. "Ah. *Æblet falder ikke langt fra stammen.* Yes, yes.

And where is your father, little girl?"

The sudden reminder of Jacob struck Juniper like a fist. "Go to hell, old man," she said.

Henriksen's eyes opened wide.

"Juniper!" Laura said. "I'm very sorry, Mr. Henriksen. There was . . . my husband was in an accident. We're still trying to deal with it."

"Ah," he said. "I didn't mean to cause you pain."

"Don't worry about it," Juniper said. "Sorry."

"It's quite all right."

"I have your letter," Laura said. "You indicated there were some things we needed to go over?"

"To business then," he said. "You received the key to the house?"

"Yes, we've been there already this morning."

"Good," Henriksen said. "Did they do an adequate job cleaning it, I wonder? I haven't had a chance to look in on the place. But please, come into my office. Your daughter is welcome to wait out here."

"She can come in with me," Laura said.

"Whatever," Juniper said. "I can probably find something less boring to do. It shouldn't be too hard to find me when you're done here."

She turned and went out. Laura watched her until the door swung shut, then shook her head and sighed. "It's been a rough few weeks."

Henriksen shrugged and smiled.

"We all have a thing that taxes us," he said. "And we are often powerless to change it."

He motioned Laura into the smaller office and closed the door behind them. A modern glass and chrome desk was situated in front of a row of tall windows that overlooked the marina. A low filing cabinet served double duty as a printer stand. The only other furnishings were two identical office chairs, one behind the desk and one in front of it. Henriksen glanced around, as if surprised by how tight the space was, then squeezed past Laura and around the desk, gesturing for her to take the matching chair.

When they were situated, Henriksen opened a folder and hunched over it, flipping through pages as he read. Laura finally cleared her throat, and he looked up at her with an apologetic smile.

"Just need to find my place here," he said. "You've taken possession of the house, and the funeral has already occurred. Not much more to talk about, but I want to be sure I don't forget anything."

"Yes," Laura said, and paused for a moment. "I was wondering how she died. Your letter wasn't very specific, and I couldn't find anything online."

"Ah," Henriksen swallowed his smile and leaned back, pulling at his lower lip. "It was . . . well, it was quite sudden. How do I say this so as not to offend? I know Americans are more sentimental about these things."

"You can just tell me," Laura said.

Henriksen narrowed his eyes. "I think you could call it a farming accident. There was very little left to bury, I'm afraid."

"What kind of farming accident?"

Henriksen sniffed and waved his hand dismissively. "An accident on a farm, of course," he said. "These things happen now and then."

"But—"

Henriksen cut her off. "I'm afraid I know very little. Let's proceed . . ."

He consulted his notes again and swiveled his chair around so he could reach the filing cabinet. He tugged on the bottom drawer and grunted, then lifted one end of the printer that sat on top of the cabinet and tried again. This time the drawer opened. He reached in and pulled out a wooden box, slammed the drawer shut and turned back around. He set the box on his desk and sat back, crossing his arms and frowning at it.

"This is it," he said. "Besides the house, I mean. This is what your mother left to you. The final bequeathment, as they say, of Charlotte Jessen."

The box was squat and ugly, it's dark surface rubbed shiny in places, and there were carvings around the edges that seemed to move in the sunlight coming through the open window. Laura leaned forward in her chair and reached out to take it, then pulled back away.

"Why wasn't this at the house?" Laura said. "Why is it in your office?"

"Charlotte kept a safe deposit box at a bank in Copenhagen. She had a key and I had a key, and when she died I opened it. This was the only thing inside."

"Why did you do that? Open it, I mean."

"Why wouldn't I? I was her lawyer and I still represent her estate—at least until you sign some papers. Believe it or not, I was quite fond of your mother and I, ah . . . I did not want anything to become public that she might have wanted to keep private."

Laura shook her head. "And you say this was the only thing she kept at the bank?"

"Aside from some cash, yes."

"And she wanted me to have it?"

"Actually, she left it for your daughter, but . . ." He broke off and tugged his lower lip some more. "I think perhaps you should be the one to decide where it goes, Mrs. Roux. To your daughter, or back to the bank, or you can burn it. No matter to me."

He leaned forward and rested his arms on the desk. "Now, as to the farm itself. The, ah, the corn was already harvested and sold, of course, but Charlotte's winter wheat will soon be coming in. Fortunately, a neighbor has agreed to help you with that."

"A neighbor?"

"Anders Karlsen. His land is adjacent to Charlotte's—to your land."

Laura smiled. "I know Anders very well, thank you."

"Good. Then all is settled. Let's get these forms signed. *Tid er penge*, after all."

• 3 •

JUNIPER WALKED to the cafe but stopped outside the door. At the long tables at the front of the dining area, the old women looked up from their gossip and pastries, and they smiled at her, their eyes sparkling with interest. One of them beckoned to her and pulled out an empty chair. Juniper scowled through the window at them, then turned and went around the corner, down the narrow alley between buildings.

Ahead, she could hear waves sloshing against the stone retaining wall, and she could taste salt in the air. She hopped up on the wall and stood, shading her eyes with her hand. Far away, a sailboat bobbed on the water, and Juniper felt a deep pang of longing. To be out there, away from everything, free to escape and explore. It sounded ideal.

Who am I kidding? she thought. She didn't know the first thing about sailboats. She could barely tread water. If she didn't drown, she would die of boredom out in the middle of the ocean.

A girl sat at the end of the pier, her back to Juniper, her feet in the water. She looked like she might be about Juniper's age, maybe a couple years older. Her hair was bright red with golden highlights that blazed in the sunlight, and she wore an old-fashioned dress, pale yellow with lace at the cuffs and throat. Juniper sat and removed her sandals, then slid down off the wall and padded out across the uneven planks of the pier. Water pooled on its weather-beaten surface, cool and delicious against the bare soles of her feet.

The girl didn't look up as she approached, and Juniper hesitated a moment before sitting and dangling her legs over the edge. She patted the water's surface with her feet, then plunged them in and gasped at the cold.

The girl finally glanced over at her, then looked away again across the little bay toward the waving fields of wheat. Juniper followed her gaze and squinted. The pier jutted out into the bay with a view of the tail end of Godhavn's curving main street and the farmland beyond. She thought she could see the peaked roof of Charlotte Jessen's barn, far away, a bright metallic glint at the tree line.

"The water's freezing," Juniper said.

"I like the cold," the girl said. Her voice was low and melodic, with a raspy undertone. "When the crops come in and the season changes, it means new possibilities. I like to think about all that empty land crusting over with frost and all the people huddled up in their little homes."

Juniper pictured the rough and rutted fields cleared of wheat and corn, the uninterrupted view of the heaving sea, and the shoreline dotted with houses, their chimneys spewing smoke into the gray sky. She shivered.

"I'm Agnes," the girl said.

"My name's Juniper."

"I know. Your mother is talking to my employer right now."

"You're the old guy's secretary?"

"His name is Kaspar," Agnes said. "I'm his assistant."

"Right," Juniper said. "He mentioned you."

"He's in love with me."

"Gross," Juniper said.

"I should say he *thinks* he's in love with me. He doesn't know the difference."

"Maybe you should get a job somewhere else."

Agnes shrugged and glanced behind them at the short row of buildings that lined the street. Juniper understood. There was nowhere else.

"How long have you lived here?"

"I've always been here," Agnes said.

"I know the feeling."

Agnes smiled. "You're from America?"

"Blue Valley," Juniper said. "Have you ever been to America?"

"Never," Agnes said.

"Blue Valley's in the middle. Flyover country, I guess."

"Is it blue?"

"It's mostly brown, but who wants to live in Brown Valley?"

"Do you miss it?"

"Not really," Juniper said. "Would you miss this place?"

"It's what I know," Agnes said.

A dead fish floated beneath them, drifting in lazy circles. Dirt spilled from a gash in its silvery skin, following the fish in muddy spirals before the water lapped it away.

"I'm sorry your grandmother died," Agnes said. "I knew her a little bit."

"I didn't know her at all. It's hard for my mom, though. She lost—well, my dad died."

"Oh," Agnes said.

"Now that Charlotte died, too, I think it's a lot for Mom."

"Then it's good she has you," Agnes said. "To comfort her."

"I guess."

A vehicle rumbled down the narrow road behind them and they both turned to watch a battered red truck as it rolled past the alleyway that divided Kaspar Henriksen's office from the bakery. Agnes shuddered and spat at the water between her feet.

"Who was that?" Juniper said. "In the truck?"

"In Blue Valley, how do you say a person is a busybody?"

"Just like that."

Agnes nodded. "That is what she is. You'll see. Stay away from her if you can."

"Whatever," Juniper said. She couldn't imagine caring.

The dead fish jerked along the surface, something nibbling at its skin from the darkness below. The water rippled and the fish vanished from sight, leaving a greasy sheen on the surface.

"This is a strange town," Juniper said.

Agnes laughed deep in her throat. "You'll get used to it."

"I won't be here long enough," Juniper said. "No offense."

Agnes looked at her for a moment, then pulled her feet out of the water. She stood and brushed off the back of her yellow dress before offering Juniper a hand. Juniper took it and Agnes pulled her up.

"You should go help your mother," Agnes said. "Kaspar isn't a bad man, but . . ."

Juniper wrinkled her nose. "Gross again," she said.

"If you get bored, I'm often here at the water, where it's cool and quiet."

"Thanks," Juniper said. "Sorry about your boss."

"He's only human," Agnes said. She shrugged again, and Juniper nodded. She walked back up the pier to the seawall and paused there to slip her sandals back on. When she looked up, Agnes was gone, and Juniper wondered if the girl had decided to take a swim.

"Brrr," she said. She turned and vaulted over the low stone wall and trudged back up the alley to look for her mother.

• 4 •

JUNIPER WAS leaning against the wall outside the law office when Laura came out. Kaspar Henriksen followed her, holding Charlotte Jessen's antique box in both hands.

"Don't forget this," he said.

Laura grimaced, but took it from him. "Of course. Thank you."

"If you want my advice," Henriksen said, "you should put it back in the bank. *Forstår du?*"

Laura tucked the box under her arm.

"I'll think about it," she said. "Thank you again, Mr. Henriksen."

Kaspar Henriksen stepped back into his office and the door swung shut. Before the latch clicked, Laura heard his voice: "*Man ligger som man har redt.*" It was almost a whisper and she wondered whether he had meant for them to hear it.

But Juniper had heard him too. Laura shook her head, her face pale.

"What was that about?" Juniper said.

"It means . . . it's sort of like 'you made your bed, now lie in it.'"

"Stupidest saying ever. What else are you supposed to do with a bed except lie in it?"

"Good point," Laura said. "Here, you carry this." Laura held out the box and Juniper took it.

"What is this?"

"It was your grandmother's. Sort of a keepsake."

"So, what did he mean?" she said. "Why was the lawyer talking about your bed?"

"I don't know, Junie."

"I don't like it here. The people are weird."

Someone cleared his throat behind them. "We're not *all* weird," he said.

Juniper jumped and turned around. A man stood on the sidewalk outside Henriksen's office, leaning on a pair of crutches. He was tall and handsome in a rugged, outdoorsy way, with a thick mane of sand-colored hair and three days' worth of stubble on his jaw. He wore a flannel shirt and jeans that had been slit open to accommodate a plaster cast on his left leg. A small boy hid behind him, clutching the man's good leg and peeking out at them with wide black eyes. It was the same boy they had seen in the wheat field.

Laura put a hand over her heart and gasped.

The man grinned. "Been a long time, Laura Loaf."

Laura clicked her tongue and looked away, then noticed Juniper and blinked as if she had forgotten her daughter was there.

"Hi," Juniper said. "I'm Laura Loaf's kid."

"*Som mor, så datter*," the man said.

"Why does everybody keep saying stuff in Danish when I know you can all speak English?"

"Sorry. I'm Anders Karlsen." Anders stuck both crutches under one arm so he could shake Juniper's hand. "I live up the road from your grandmother's house. This is my son, Magnus."

The boy butted his head against Anders's leg like a shy goat.

"I saw you before," Juniper said. "Were you following us?"

The boy stared at Juniper from behind his father and—

for just a second—she thought she saw a dark shape slither past behind his eyes, flicking away like a fish in a dirty tank.

"Anders and I went to school together," Laura said. "It's been years."

"Not my fault. You left, I stayed."

"It's not my fault you stayed."

Anders took a moment to maneuver both crutches under his arms, then cleared his throat again. "Listen, I was sorry to hear about your mom."

"Thank you."

"I told Henriksen I'd be happy to help out with the harvest."

"I wouldn't want to put you to the trouble. I'm sure we can hire someone."

"Oh, it's no trouble. I did a lot of the planting up there. It's been a tough couple years. Hotter summer means a shorter season and a smaller yield. More bugs, too. Charlotte had her hands full."

Laura leaned toward him and put her hand out, but then drew it back and folded her arms across her chest.

"Well, I'm glad she had you there," she said. "Since Dad died, I've been worried about her being alone."

"Oh, she wasn't alone," Anders said. "She had—" He glanced at Juniper, then back at Laura so quickly that she wondered whether she had imagined the sudden misery in his eyes.

"She had company."

"Company?" Laura said. "Oh."

There was an awkward silence, and Juniper grimaced at the boy, widening her eyes.

Magnus smiled and kicked at his father's cast, creating a hollow thud that broke the tension.

"Ow!" Anders said. "What was that for?"

Magnus shrugged.

"I'm sorry," Laura said. "I didn't even ask about your leg. What happened?"

"One of those things," Anders said. "I guess I'm not as young as I used to be, huh?"

"Me neither."

"Maybe," Anders said, "but you still look amazing."

Juniper turned and started walking down the street.

"We'd better get back," she said over her shoulder. "Still lots of unpacking to do, Mom."

"Right," Laura said. "It was good running into you, Anders."

"Sure," he said. "Seriously, as soon as I get out of this cast, I'll bring in your crop. I mean it. It's no trouble."

"Thanks. We'll talk later, okay?"

Laura jogged to make up the distance to her daughter. When she drew even, Juniper handed the box back.

"You can carry this for a while. It's heavy."

Laura took it, and they walked back to the path and across the field in silence. Far ahead, they could see the roof of the yellow farmhouse, and beyond that, a flat gray line at the horizon. Juniper imagined the ocean churning and foaming at some unseen shore, and it made her shiver.

"You used to date that guy, huh?" she said.

"Junie, could you just for once . . ." Laura began, but she didn't finish her thought. She and Juniper walked on through the high rustling stalks without another word.

• 5 •

THE WOODEN FLOOR sagged and creaked in her grand-mother's room, and the wind under the eaves whispered. Juniper pulled off her overalls and shirt and examined her body in the mirror on the back of Charlotte's closet door. In her matching pink panties and camisole she looked nude if she crossed her eyes a little and blurred herself. She traced the puckered scars on her thighs with a fingertip. She had found matches and a small box of razor blades in the upstairs bathroom while Laura was exploring the kitchen, and now she felt around under the mattress. She pulled one of the blades free and ran her thumb across its sharp edge, delighting in the newness of it. She would eventually have to find a better hiding place for her contraband, but the mattress would do for a while. She didn't think her mother would search the room in front of her.

They were supposed to be building trust.

She placed the flat of the blade against her thigh. The cold metal gave her goosebumps. She watched light play on its bright steel surface, then tipped the lamp on the dresser and slid the blade beneath its heavy base. It was comforting to know it was nearby.

She sat on the bed and reached for her overalls, idly scratching her ankle. She felt a stabbing pain and pulled her hand back, momentarily afraid she was still holding the razor blade. She held her leg out in front of her and turned her ankle so she could see it in the dim old-lady light of the standing lamp. A long brown caterpillar with an ornate design on its back moved slowly up her calf. The worm oozed along another fraction of an inch as she watched—fascinated and frozen—and it bit down again.

She yelped and grabbed the insect. Pinching it between her thumb and finger, she pulled it off her leg. Holding it at arm's length, she ran to the door and yanked it open.

"Mom!"

She heard Laura's footsteps cross the living room and mount the stairs. Juniper retreated to the bed and dropped the worm into a cup on the nightstand, closing her hand over it as if it might jump out.

Laura appeared at the door, her head cocked to one side, eyebrows raised.

"A worm bit me," Juniper said.

"Worms don't bite."

Juniper held out the cup, opening her fingers so her mother could see the thing. Laura crossed to the bed and sat next to her daughter. She bent and examined the caterpillar, which writhed around, trying to climb the steep walls of the cup. A pinprick of dark liquid still clung to its skin.

"That's a cutworm," Laura said. "They grow up to be moths. Your grandma obviously had an infestation."

"We should call an exterminator."

"This one, though—this one might have come from the field when we crossed it. From the crops. Maybe it was on your clothes."

"It was on my leg. Crawling around and trying to eat me."

"Eat you?"

"It bit me. I'm bleeding."

"Let me see."

Juniper laid back and waved her leg in her mother's face. In the dim light the smear of blood along her ankle looked thick and black. Laura stood up and took a step back.

"It feasts on human flesh," Juniper said. "A monster in the form of a worm. The Old Gods rise, and humanity is doomed. Doomed!"

Laura shook her head and left the room. Juniper sat back up, dumping the worm out onto the table beside her. The patterns on its back shifted as its lumpy little body twisted, untangling and righting itself. When Laura returned, she was carrying a brown bottle of peroxide and a small box of adhesive bandages with a Danish brand name. As she tended to Juniper's leg, she glanced at the caterpillar inching across the dusty surface of the dresser. She shook her head again and muttered something to herself.

"What?" Juniper said.

"Nothing," Laura said.

"No, what?"

"Cutworms eat plants," Laura said. "Not people. They can destroy whole crops, but I've never heard of one biting anybody."

"This one's special, I guess."

"I guess so."

The doorbell rang downstairs and they both jumped, startled by the sudden chime echoing through the big, empty house.

"Who could that be?"

Before she left the room, Laura picked the cutworm up from the dresser. A minute later, Juniper heard the toilet flush in the bathroom, then her mother's footsteps on the stairs. Juniper reached for her overalls, balled up on the floor next to the bed, and shook them out. Another cutworm tumbled out across the worn hardwood planks. She scooped it up and held it close to her face.

"Hello, little friend," Juniper said. "Let's play a game."

It curled into a ball in her palm and Juniper smiled. She reached for the table lamp and the blade hidden under its base.

• 6 •

THERE WAS a dead bird on the doorstep.

Laura checked to make sure Juniper hadn't followed her, then stepped outside and quietly closed the door behind her. She scanned the landscape—the fields of waving wheat, the ugly metal barn, the blackened circle on the ground, and the distant tree line—and saw nothing out of the ordinary. She decided the bird had flown into the door jamb and hit the bell before falling to the ground and dying.

It looked like a young magpie, roughly the size of Laura's hand, black and white with a shimmering green streak. Its beak was open, and its dull black eye stared up at the sky. She turned to go back in, intending to fetch the broom, but saw the bird move in her peripheral vision. She stopped and turned.

The bird flapped one wing and rolled onto its back. It turned its head and looked at her with its dead eye, its beak opening and closing. Then, like a clockwork tin soldier winding down, its movements grew feeble. The flapping of its wings slowed, then stopped.

She picked up a stick and reached out to poke the bird. A fat white worm popped out from under a wing and wiggled away, tumbling out of sight over the edge of the porch.

Laura kneeled and prodded the bird's body, then dragged

it toward her. It turned under the stick, a dark streak following it over the smooth flagstones.

She felt like a child, aware that she was doing something strange and not sure why she *was* doing it—but doing it anyway. The bird was there and she was there and she wanted to see it better.

She gave the bird a final poke and something popped—she could feel it through the length of the stick. The bird's abdomen opened up, maggots spilling out and squirming away in every direction, blindly seeking safety. The skin of the bird was packed with dirt and insects and old leaves. Laura gasped, but couldn't stop watching as some of the maggots writhed toward her, moist and white, tumbling into the cracks between the stones.

She didn't hear tires crunching on the gravel drive or a truck door slamming or boots scuffing up the walkway.

"Oh, how dreadful."

Startled, Laura looked up and saw an old woman standing six feet away from her. The woman was holding two plastic containers with thick rubber lids. She was dressed in khakis and a canvas jacket, and a giant straw hat shadowed her craggy face. A wisp of gray hair had come loose, and it fluttered in the breeze along the hat's brim like a groping tentacle.

"How dreadful," the woman said again. "You really shouldn't touch that. It doesn't look clean."

"I think someone put this here," Laura said.

"It could've got here on its own," the woman said. "You never know."

She set the covered dishes on the railing post and frowned at the bird's desecrated body, then took a step forward and kicked it hard out over the steps. The bird bounced and rolled away into the long grass.

"We should bury it," Laura said.

"You'll have to burn it," the woman said. "Sooner or later." The woman waved her hand at nothing in particular

and then stuck it out for Laura to take. She pulled Laura to her feet and leaned down to brush off the knees of Laura's jeans. Laura found the gesture overly familiar, but somehow comforting.

"I'm afraid the children around here get bored sometimes," the woman said. "They pull little pranks to amuse themselves, but they mean no harm. It's usually best to ignore them. I'm Anna, by the way. I live up the road a couple miles."

"I'm sorry," Laura said. "I was just—"

"Surprised? Disgusted? Can't say I blame you. I would be, too, if I hadn't seen it before."

"I'm Laura. Laura Roux. Charlotte Jessen was my mother." She pointed up at the house as if Charlotte might still be inside.

"Oh, Charlotte talked about you all the time," Anna said.

"You knew my mother?"

"I knew her very well. We went swimming most mornings. Your mother was a lousy swimmer, but she enjoyed the exercise and I enjoyed her company." Anna turned and grabbed the dishes she had brought. She held them out and Laura took them.

"Thank you," Laura said.

"It's nothing much, but it occurred to me you might not have had time to lay in any food and I wasn't sure what Charlotte still had in the house." She winked conspiratorially. "For all her qualities, your mother wasn't one of the great cooks."

"You're a lifesaver," Laura said. "We meant to pick up some groceries in town, but I got sidetracked and forgot. Only some crackers and a couple jars of herring left in the kitchen. Dinner was gonna be pretty grim tonight."

Anna laughed, a light sound that reminded Laura of faraway chimes.

"Can't have that," Anna said. "I'd have invited you for a proper meal, but I didn't want to be a nuisance."

"Once I stock the pantry we'll have you over," Laura said.

"As long as herring isn't on the menu. You said *we*—is your husband with you?"

Laura felt her smile fade and she took a deep breath. "Just me and my daughter, Juniper."

Anna gazed at Laura's face for a long moment, then nodded. "I'm so sorry, Laura. I'm an old fool. I knew about your husband and I forgot."

"It's okay. I forget sometimes, too. I'm still getting used to it."

"It'll take a little time, and it will always hurt, but maybe not as much as it does right now." Anna shook her head and flashed a rueful smile. "So, tell me. How long are you staying? Are you my new neighbor or is this just a quick jaunt to the old farm?"

There was an underlying insensitivity to the question. After all, they were only there because Laura's mother had died. But Anna's bluntness didn't seem malicious. Laura glanced at the house again, worried that Juniper could hear them.

"We might stay for a while," she said.

"And how long is a while?"

Laura shrugged. "Indefinitely?"

Anna clapped her hands. "Tell me, do you swim?"

"Not very well."

"Like mother, like daughter. You must come with me some morning."

"I'll look you up as soon as we're settled."

"Do that. I look forward to meeting your girl."

Anna glanced up at the windows of the house and a cloud seemed to pass over her face. Then she smiled again, tapped the heels of her boots together and retreated down the porch steps. She hopped into her bright red truck and waved out the window before backing away down the drive.

Laura looked out at the wild yard, but the body of the poor magpie was lost in the long grass. Laura hefted the plastic containers, and when she turned to go back into the house she looked up and saw a curtain flick across one of the windows. She hoped Juniper hadn't overheard her conversation with Anna. She still hadn't figured out how to break the news that they were staying.

At least they weren't stuck with herring for dinner.

• 7 •

JUNIPER SAT at the end of Charlotte's bed and watched dust motes drift across the soft light coming through the curtains. Her mother hadn't mentioned that they might be stuck in Jutland permanently. Laura had treated the whole trip like a vacation.

Juniper's suitcase was on the floor, butted up against the wall and standing open. Some of her clothes were draped over the side, and her toiletries bag was unzipped and sitting on top of a shoebox crammed with three pairs of shoes. She had only packed for a week in Godhavn, and now she wondered what was to become of the rest of her things, her entire life.

After the accident, her mother had kept her home for weeks. Laura had turned visitors away and arranged for Juniper's teachers to email her assignments. At the time, Juniper had felt grateful. She couldn't muster the energy to connect with another person.

She had been emptied out.

Juniper had not had a real conversation with anyone but her mother in weeks, and now she was being robbed of the opportunity to say goodbye to her friends, to take a last tour of the house, or to visit her father's grave. She thought there ought to have been some discussion, some warning, if they were never going to return.

And yet she couldn't muster much anger toward her

mother. Starting over in a new place—where nobody knew her, where nobody would ever pity her or blame her for her father's death—would be a relief. She would never have to experience that moment of confusion when she came home from school and the car wasn't in the driveway, would never have to smell her father's lingering aftershave in a room, would never wonder where he was before realizing he was nowhere at all.

But did that mean he would disappear from her memory faster? Which was worse, the loss or the constant reminder of the loss?

Her grandmother's antique box sat on the dresser, and on an impulse she rose, grabbed it, and returned to the bed. The box was made of dark wood, roughly eight by twelve inches and four inches deep, stained and polished, worn around the corners. It was covered with ornate scrollwork, and Juniper could almost read the story on its surface. Intricately carved trees and stalks of corn on the side closest to her gave way to the rudimentary shapes of farmers gathering at the front of the box with rakes and pitchforks. Under the clasp was a depiction of a bonfire, and across from the farmers were three young women. Their faces were crude, their mouths tiny circles, and their arms were outstretched, as if they were defending themselves from the fire. One of them had her back turned, and her torso was hollow. Tree branches grew from the hole in her back, and leaves spilled from her onto the ground. Behind the women the crops shrank, and the trees became bare as crosshatched clouds appeared along the top corner. The lid was attached to the body of the chest with tiny brass hinges and a brass latch with a keyhole. She wondered if Mr. Henriksen had given her mother a key. There was a narrow gap under the lid where the wood had warped over time. Juniper got back up and opened the drawers of the wardrobe, looking for any kind of flat metal object long enough to reach the catch inside the box, but all she found were socks and underwear and her grandmother's costume jewelry.

She considered getting a knife from the kitchen, but she was reasonably certain her mother had hidden the knives already. She went to the closet, hoping for an old shoe horn or a belt buckle she could repurpose, but instead found a rack of men's clothing: overalls and jeans and a single dark suit covered in plastic, a dry cleaner's ticket still taped to the wire hanger. She took the suit out of the closet and pulled it off the hanger, letting it drop to the floor, then uncrimped the wire and reshaped the hanger, bending it in half and twisting it into a crude tool.

She jammed the sharp end of the hanger into the gap under the box's lid and wiggled it back and forth until she heard a faint click. With a soft whoop of triumph, she lifted the tiny latch and raised the lid. She swept the palm of her hand across the center of the bed, smoothing Charlotte's duvet, and laid the contents of the box in neat rows as she emptied it.

There was a doll made of cornhusks and twine; an old pipe, its mouthpiece chewed down to a nub; a dried rodent paw that may have once belonged to a squirrel or rabbit; a lock of gray hair tied with green ribbon; a leather-bound journal, roughly the size of a datebook, its pages stained and yellow, its cover cracked and rough; and at the bottom of the chest, under the book, two photographs, one black and white, small and square, with scalloped white edges, the other a thin color printout, hand-cut from a larger piece of laser paper.

Juniper ignored the other items and squinted at the old photo. It depicted a couple standing in front of the farmhouse, smiling at the camera. The man leaned on a real estate placard that read SOLGT. She recognized the woman as her grandmother and she assumed the man was her grandfather, both of them young and just starting out, having bought a little yellow house they would live in for the rest of their lives. At the edge of the photo, Juniper could see part of the barn

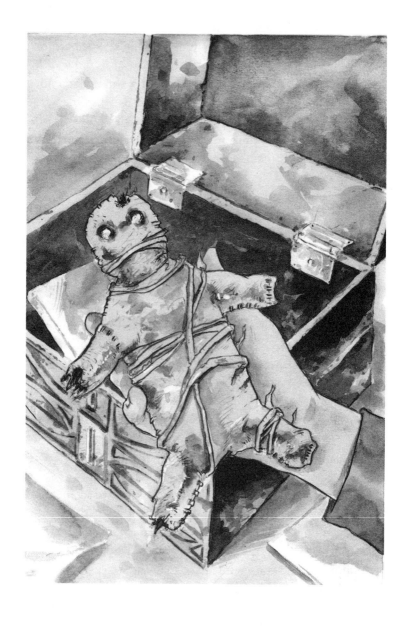

(old and wooden, not yet torn down to make room for the modern hangar-style barn that would replace it) and, behind that, tall rows of wheat.

She set the portrait against the side of the box so she could still see it while she examined the color printout. In the new picture her grandmother was more recognizable, closer to the age Juniper remembered from the handful of times she had seen her. Charlotte's carefully coiffed hair was sprayed into place, her posture stiff with age, her expression joyous.

Beside her stood the same young man from the older photo, shirtless and squinting into the sun. Charlotte had her arm around his waist, and he was leaning against the handle of a scythe—his stance the same as it was in the black and white image—as if he had taken a break from working in the fields to have his picture taken.

Juniper frowned, puzzled. She set the color printout next to the little square photograph and studied them. She was sure the young woman was Charlotte Jessen. She had aged perhaps forty years between posing for the camera each time. But the man looked exactly the same in both pictures. If it wasn't her grandfather in the color printout, it must surely be a close relative. The way Charlotte held the young man around his waist implied a level of intimacy that Juniper found disturbing.

What was their relationship? And who had taken the pictures?

She considered showing the photos to her mother, but Laura was keeping secrets. She hadn't told Juniper they were never going home to Blue Valley. Would she be willing to talk openly about Charlotte's relationship with a younger man who looked just like her dead husband? Juniper shook her head as if the question had been asked aloud.

The cornhusk doll, the dried animal paw, and the lock of hair were intriguing, but none of them meant much of anything without some context. She gathered the three objects up and tossed them back in the box.

The only thing left was the leather journal. Juniper was cautiously optimistic that it would provide the answers she was looking for, but part of her hoped it wouldn't. She was starting to concoct a vague mystery in which her lonely grandmother had been seduced by a traveling con man who resembled Tor Jessen.

She peeled back the cracked cover of the book and riffled through its pages. Watery gray symbols marched in uneven lines across the first few pages. They reminded Juniper of a boy she had kissed at a party. He had shown her his tattoo: Viking runes inked on his skinny bicep. He had told her the symbols meant *Passionate Lover*, but she later heard him tell a boy they meant *Great Warrior*. Either way, they had looked like gibberish to her. She flipped the pages, disappointed, but on the second to last page, was a passage written in English. The handwriting was feminine, but shaky.

There were still rows of runes on the page, but each line had been translated beneath in darker black ink. More designs ran around the edges of the page: twisted leering faces, suns and moons, and ears of corn. Juniper brought the book closer to the lamp and ignored the runes and drawings, her lips moving as she read the words she could understand:

HØST HULDER

First to the earth, from the dark before all time, from the dark beyond all sight, came the Old Ones. From Their will the Old Ones brought forth the seasons to the land. In spring They trod the barren fields and spread Their seed, and thus in the summer came the People. And as the People were made to serve the needs of the Old Ones, so too did the People plant the crops of wheat and of corn for their own needs. Then, in the autumn, many of the People were sundered in the harvest, and the Old Ones withdrew under the earth. Through the emptiness of winter the remaining People were unfulfilled, but the spring came again and with it came the return of their crops, and so the People survived. To reap the harvest, they made in their image the Høst Hulder, and in it lived the spirits of the Old Ones. Through the Hulder the Old Ones looked upon the People, and the Hulder labored through all the long days of the summer. But in the shadows of autumn, the Hulder must itself be culled and the grain gathered to last through winter. Thus will it be until the end of the Old Ones's dreamless sleep, and the People themselves will feed the hunger of waking giants.

Juniper glanced at the door, wondering where her mother was, then turned the page. There were more English words, interspersed with what looked like Danish, with each stanza of a poem translated beneath it:

at indkalde
(Der skal afgives et tilbud.)

An offering must be made.

Den elskede (en lighed).
Blod. (brænd til aske).

Et bidrag (fra marken).

The loved one (a likeness in flames).
Blood (become ashes).
A contribution (from the field).

Fra denne lighed.
Med dette blod.
Jeg accepterer byrden.

From this likeness.
With this blood.
I accept the burden.

Fra denne andrager.
Med denne hyldest.
Jeg accepterer sorg.

From this petitioner.
With this tribute.
I accept the sorrow.

Fra kærlighed.
Med smerte.
Jeg afventer.

From love.
With agony.
I wait.

Juniper felt certain the English version of the poem had been written by her grandmother, but she didn't understand what it meant. Had it been some sort of strange love letter to the mysterious younger man?

She heard the front door close and floorboards creak as her mother moved around downstairs.

"Junie? You up there?"

"Getting ready to take a shower, Mom!"

"Hurry up. A neighbor brought us dinner."

"I'll be down in a few minutes, okay?"

More floorboards creaked as her mother moved past the base of the stairs, headed toward the kitchen.

Juniper jumped up from the bed and tipped back the table lamp. Her razor blade was still hidden beneath the base. She creased the last page of the journal and sliced it out of the book. She folded the thick, yellowed paper twice and slid it under her mattress. Then she put the book and the photographs back in the box and took it to her mother's room. She left it on the table next to the bed before retreating to the bathroom and turning on the water in the shower.

She still didn't think much of Godhavn, but now she had a mystery to think about. And a distraction from the memories that had followed her halfway around the world.

• 8 •

THE TUPPERWARE DISHES contained pork chops and smashed potatoes with peas. Laura heated the food in the oven and they ate at the tiny kitchen table. The meat was dry, and Juniper got up and went to the drawers under the counter. Laura watched her, waiting for the inevitable question or angry blow-up, but after a minute Juniper quietly closed the drawers and came back to the table. She picked up her pork chop and ate it with her fingers. In a show of solidarity, Laura did the same.

When the dishes were washed and sitting in the strainer to dry, they turned on the television in the front room. They tuned in to an episode of a show they'd never heard of, but neither of them paid much attention to it. Juniper kept looking up from the screen, casting her gaze around the unfamiliar room, and Laura watched her from the corner of her eye. Finally, Juniper stood and walked over to the photographs that lined the hallway. She peered closely at each of them before moving on to the next. Finally she stopped and pointed at one of the bigger pictures, framed in gold in the center of a grouping.

"This is Grandpa and Grandma, right?"

Laura turned off the TV and came to stand next to her.

"Their thirtieth anniversary," she said. "You were still little so we couldn't make it over here that year."

The memory brought a twinge of sadness. Jacob had offered to stay home with Juniper, had encouraged Laura to go celebrate her parents' anniversary, but Junie had been so little, so dependent, the thought of leaving her was unthinkable. Now that tiny creature was gone, and so was Jacob. So were Laura's parents. The world changed so quickly.

"So they were old already," Juniper said. "But I don't see any pictures of them when they were young."

"No?"

She squinted at the long line of framed photographs that receded into the darkness of the foyer. There were pictures of Laura at various ages, including one in her Communion dress standing next to Anders, who looked young and cocky in his blue suit. There were a few pictures of people Laura didn't recognize, but Juniper was right. There was only one picture of Charlotte and Tor—in their early sixties, sitting at a table in front of a sheet cake covered with candles.

"I guess maybe—wait."

She went to the bookcase next to the television and kneeled down to get at the bottom shelf. There, next to a handful of dusty DVDs, some cookbooks, and an accordion file of old appliance manuals, were two thick photo albums, one green and one red, with gold filigree patterns along the spines. She pulled them out and took them to the couch, and Juniper came and sat beside her. Laura opened the red one. It was filled with her own wedding pictures and Juniper's school pictures. She closed it and set it aside, then opened the green album on her lap.

It was older, with black and white photos pasted into the first few pages, giving way a few pages later to faded Polaroids fastened with mounting corners.

"Here they are," she said.

She pointed at a photograph taken some time in the sixties or seventies. Charlotte and Tor stood side by side in front of the house they had just purchased and would spend the rest of their lives in. Tor was grinning at the camera, his chin out, a stalk of wheat jutting from his teeth.

"Good ol' Farmer Bob," Juniper said.

"What?"

"Nothing," Juniper said. "So that's Grandpa? Your dad?"

"Before I was even a glint."

"How old do you think he was there?"

"I don't know," Laura said. "Maybe twenty-five? Thirty? I'd like to visit their graves tomorrow. Would you go with me?"

"I guess. But did Grandpa have, like, kids from a previous marriage? Or maybe a much younger cousin who looked just like him?"

"What? Why?"

"Just making conversation. God, I thought you wanted to talk about stuff."

"I do. I just . . . I don't understand."

"I want to know more about my family, that's all. I never even met my grandpa. Is it so wrong to ask questions about him?"

"No," Laura said, "it's not wrong." She took another look at the photo. Her mother's face was unlined, sunlight in her pale hair. The Jessens were still childless; their only cares and worries revolved around a house, a farm, and each other.

"And, no," she said. "I don't think your grandfather had a lot of close relatives. Neither did your grandma. They were alone out here when they started out."

She wasn't sure Juniper had heard her. She was staring into space with a puzzled expression. Then she shook her head and stood up. She stretched and looked down at her mother, and for just a second Laura saw something cold—hostile—in her daughter's eyes.

"I'm going to bed," Juniper said.

"I'll be up in a bit," Laura said. "You okay in your grandma's room?"

"Yeah, I like it in there. It feels old."

"That's a good thing?"

Juniper shrugged and went up the stairs without saying goodnight. Laura almost hollered after her, almost reminded her to brush her teeth. But Juniper would be just as likely to skip brushing her teeth if she were reminded. She didn't need her mother's help and didn't want it most of the time.

Laura skimmed through the rest of the green album, stopping here and there to gaze at a picture of her father at work in a field, her mother hanging clothes to dry in the sun. Her parents had moved to the middle of nowhere, bought a farm, and raised a child. Tor and Charlotte had started out with no one, found each other, and created something new. But then Laura had moved away to America, Tor had died, and Charlotte had been alone in the world again.

Laura feared she was following in her mother's footsteps.

• 9 •

KASPAR HENRIKSEN closed the tabs on his browser and stacked some of the papers that were scattered on his desk. Most of them had to do with the Jessen estate, and that matter was now closed as far as he was concerned. He had tried to warn Laura Roux of the danger she was in, speaking in Danish, a language the daughter did not understand. If she chose not to follow his advice, that was her own concern.

He labeled a new Manila folder and placed the paperwork in it, tapped the edges straight and lifted the printer so he could stick the folder in his cabinet between files marked IBSEN and JOHANSEN. He turned off the desk lamp, pushed his chair in, and left, closing the inner door behind him.

Agnes was not at her desk in the lobby. She had left another squirrel on the floor by the front door. He sighed and picked it up by its tail, carried it to the wastebasket and dropped it in.

Henriksen was sixty-eight years old. He had never been married nor felt any desire to marry, had never sired a child, and had avoided emotional entanglements for most of his adult life. He had focused on his career to the exclusion of all other concerns—except one. He had fallen in love with his secretary. He had not known how to express his feelings, and so he had kept them to himself.

Outside the air was chilly, and he stopped on the sidewalk

to button his coat. The fresh air felt good after the musty office. He sniffed and smelled burning wood. At the mouth of the alley he looked down at the boats in the little bay. He sometimes wondered what it would be like to take one of them and sail away forever.

A figure stood in the shadows at the end of the pier. He recognized the slope of her shoulders and the moonlit sparkle of red in her hair.

"Agnes?" he said.

She did not turn around, so he walked down the alley and through the opening in the low seawall to the end of the pier. Agnes stood motionless, looking out at the water.

"Agnes," he said. "Dear?"

She glanced at him, then looked back at the horizon, and he followed her gaze. Someone had a bonfire going in a field across the bay, and Henriksen took another sniff. It smelled like childhood and comfort and tradition. It smelled like endings.

"Agnes, are you all right?"

She ignored him so he reached out, almost put his hand on her shoulder, but then thought better of it and pulled back. She looked at him again, her black eyes unreadable, her lips drawn back in a snarl. A runner of spit dangled from her chin like an anchor. He could now see that her hair was tangled, greasy curls clinging to her forehead and cheeks.

She moved toward him and he took a reflexive step back. The thought came— inappropriate to the moment— that they were finally dancing, something he had often dreamed about.

Their tango continued down the length of the pier, back toward the seawall, Agnes lurching toward him in fitful spurts as he walked backward, his hands out as if he could calm her or hold her at bay.

Hold her at bay on the bay, he thought. He wondered if he was becoming hysterical.

She growled and crouched, then leapt at him, her fingers twisted into claws as she reached for his throat. He surprised himself by charging forward, a scream rising from somewhere deep in his chest. He barreled into her and she fell, her fingernails ripping a chunk of skin from the palm of his left hand.

There was a piling behind her, and he heard something crunch under her skin when she hit it. She bounced off and back toward him. The piling had cut her. Black liquid, glittering in the moonlight, seeped down her side, soaking into her filthy dress and dripping onto the surface of the dock. Disgusted, he lashed out again, and again she was caught off balance. Her ankle turned, and she tumbled sideways into the water. There was a loud splash, and she disappeared from view.

He held his breath, counting the seconds in his head, waiting to see if she would drag herself up onto the dock. Finally he stepped to the edge and peered over it. The sea churned and foamed, but there was no sign of Konrad Henriksen's secretary. She had sunk or had perhaps been carried away by the tide.

"Oh, Agnes," he said.

He dropped to his knees. Cold water instantly soaked through the thin fabric of his trousers, but he didn't feel it. He buried his face in his bloody hands and began to cry.

• 10 •

HER DREAM began in the big church parking lot on 167th Street, just north of Black Forest Estates. Juniper had practically begged her father to let her practice driving on the church's cracked and empty blacktop, but he insisted she get experience on the road. As he had that day in real life, he let her take a few turns around the lot, then pointed to the exit and waggled his eyebrows at her. She took a deep breath, looked both ways, and eased their old Subaru out onto the two-lane country road.

"Signal," Jacob Roux said to his daughter. "Don't forget, nobody knows what you're going to do unless you tell them."

Juniper gritted her teeth and nodded. Her hands were in the ten-and-two positions, fighting each other a little, the wheel wobbling back and forth as she worked to keep the car straight.

"Check your mirrors," Jacob said.

"I already did," Juniper said, but she glanced in the rear-view anyway.

"Good."

"Is the instructor gonna scold me the whole time?"

"Probably not. They'll be silently judging you."

"Oh, great. That totally sets my mind at ease."

"Your mind's not supposed to be at ease," Jacob said. "You're supposed to be concentrating."

When she looked over at him, he was smiling.

The Subaru smelled dusty and hot. Jacob and Laura had bought a new hybrid and put the Subaru in storage, to be passed along to Juniper the day she turned sixteen. It had been the family car for as long as Juniper could remember. There was a purple stain on the backseat where her crayons had melted in the sun. Old cracker crumbs were mashed deep into the seams of the upholstery, and a small rip decorated the headliner where Laura had transported tomato cages in the passenger seat. Jacob had worried that the car wouldn't start, that it had sat too long, but the Subaru roared instantly to life when Juniper turned the key in the ignition, and they both whooped with joy.

"Look at that," Jacob said. "The old girl's got some life in her yet."

Juniper had spent ten minutes brushing cobwebs off the car before backing it out of the garage and carefully wending her way through town to the church, her father giving her directions despite the fact that she had spent her entire life riding bicycles and skateboards over every inch of every sidewalk and street.

Leaving the parking lot behind, Juniper felt a thrill of adrenaline and a spike of chilly fear. It was hard to imagine she would ever take driving for granted the way her parents did, unthinkable that she would ever have the casual confidence required to slide into the driver's seat without steeling her nerves first.

The landscape around them was all scrubby weeds and volunteer trees. Juniper glanced down at the speedometer every few seconds, keeping the car at a steady thirty miles an hour as they passed isolated brick houses set back behind painted fences and swaths of freshly mowed grass. An orange moving truck came up fast behind them and slowed, then moved into the other lane and blew past.

A minute later, the fencing abruptly came to an end and

they were in a dark green tunnel formed from the overhanging branches of old oak trees. The air was thick with dust and pollen kicked up by the truck, now an orange speck far ahead of them.

She veered a few inches toward the yellow line and yanked the wheel a little too hard, yawing toward a weedy ditch and then back again to the middle of the lane. She let out a shaky breath and leaned forward, causing the seatbelt to snug up tight against her chest.

"Take it easy," Jacob said. "Imagine you're on your bike or the longboard. The car will only do what you tell it to. You're in charge."

"That's what I'm afraid of," Juniper said.

Jacob chuckled and Juniper felt a flash of annoyance. She looked over at him, trying to think of a way to express her irritation that wouldn't cause an argument. She and her father had been getting along much better the last few weeks, and she didn't want to upset their détente.

Jacob looked straight ahead, his right arm outstretched, his hand on the dash. "Watch the road," he said. "Watch the road!"

She looked ahead and saw a deer blocking the road, watching their approach. For the next few seconds the car seemed to move in slow motion, dust swirling away and freezing in place, and Juniper was able to take in a surprising amount of detail, even as her foot came off the accelerator and stabbed instinctively at the brake pedal.

The buck was roughly five feet tall, his chest and neck a solid wall of muscle. His rack was nearly as wide as the Subaru and seemed impossibly heavy for any animal to carry. His eyes were brown and moist; his wide nose was jet black. Juniper could imagine his taut muscles under the palm of her hand, his sleek coat bristling in the breeze.

Then he moved.

Lightning strikes and the statue springs to life.

The brake pedal finally responded to pressure from her foot. The family car shuddered and stopped, throwing her against the seatbelt and flinging her father forward against the dash. She heard his elbow snap as the buck bounded, not away into the woods but toward them, straight down the yellow line. He charged at the Subaru and leapt into the air a second before impact.

His hooves shattered the windshield, the sound of breaking glass drowning out Jacob Roux's scream. The buck was screaming too, his hooves flailing about in the confines of the Subaru's cab, his impressive rack somehow in the car with them, thrashing back and forth. The car horn was blaring and the Subaru was rolling. Juniper could feel it moving beneath her, but she couldn't reach the pedals. She pushed out with her foot again and again, but her limbs felt heavy and she couldn't move her leg far enough. She pulled at the door handle, desperate to get out of the car, away from the chaos, but the seatbelt held her. She looked down, trying to find the buckle, but there were antlers everywhere, an aerial view of a winter forest. There were antlers buried deep in the upholstery.

There were antlers buried deep in Juniper's chest.

Blood spattered across her face and she tried to lift her arm to wipe it away, but the deer's head was in her lap, pinning her down. He looked up at her, panic in his big brown eyes.

She turned her head and saw her father slumped beside her, his left arm twisted awkwardly across the console between them, and she understood that his last act had been to reach out—to protect her from the impact. Jacob Roux's jaw hung loose, and the right side of his chest was laid open, a twitching hoof tangled in his ribs. Juniper watched his heart beat once, and again, then stop.

She screamed, and the deer jerked and the antlers twisted, and the world disappeared in a flash of white pain.

She woke up in her grandmother's room and turned on the table lamp. She was alone. Her father was gone, her wounds were scars. She felt certain she would spend the rest of her life dreaming about her father's death.

She left the lamp on and watched the curtains billow in the breeze. They undulated like water, and she felt her eyes grow heavy and close again.

This time her sleep was dreamless.

• 11 •

A SOUND WOKE HER, and Juniper had the immediate and instinctual feeling that someone was nearby, that she was being watched in the darkness of the strange room. She lay quietly with her eyes open wide, listening for anything out of the ordinary. It was her first night in an umfamiliar place, and she knew there had to be normal sounds that she wasn't used to.

She rolled off the bed and crouched beside it, watching the open closet. She was certain the sound had come from behind the dusty rack of her dead grandfather's clothing.

The black suit was still crumpled on the floor, and Juniper crawled over it, trying to see into the darkest shadows at the back of the closet. She kneeled on the ruined wire hanger and almost gasped in pain, but clamped her mouth shut and picked up the twisted length of wire. She squeezed the two halves together and the tension in the wire pushed them back against the palm of her hand. The pressure felt comforting.

She held still, listening, squeezing the hanger, until she heard the sound again, low and muffled, like someone breathing. She reversed the bent hanger in her hand and, holding it like a dagger, she leapt forward. She used her free hand to find a gap between the jeans and the pressed white shirts, sweeping them aside so she could see the back of the closet.

Four feet up from the floor was a perfectly round hole, a black dot in the middle of the white wall. And then the dot blinked, and she realized there was an eye behind the hole.

The eye looked directly at her.

Juniper thrust the jagged ends of the hanger through the hole, and the person on the other side of the wall shrieked. It occurred to her too late that it might have been Laura's eye, and she was relieved that the screaming voice sounded nothing like her mother's.

She pulled the hanger back and felt a slight bit of resistance as it came free. She fell, landing on the pile of clothing, and scrambled backward as something oozed out of the darkness behind the hole.

A black tentacle groped along the wall, then pushed out into the room. It was smooth and suckerless, and it glistened in the wan moonlight. A second tentacle pushed past the first, through the hole and along the floor. It slithered over the uneven wood and under Tor Jessen's Sunday suit, causing the jacket to ripple and scoot toward Juniper. She crab-walked away until the top of her head hit the side of the bed and there was nowhere left to go.

Her breath came in panicked gasps and her neck felt so stiff she thought it might break. But when the tip of the tentacle wriggled out from under the suit coat and touched the bottom of her foot, Juniper screamed and rolled away. She jumped over the questing thing on the floor and ran to the closet door, slamming it shut against the bulging tentacles. There was another shriek from behind the wall, and she slammed the door again, as hard as she could. The tentacles pushed against it, then retreated, squirming back into the closet. She opened the door again, ready to slam it shut a third time, and saw that both tentacles were shriveling into the hole, squeezing back through the small opening.

Juniper ran out into the hallway. The door to the linen closet stood open and she went to it, sidling along the wall until she could peek inside. Empty.

She heard footsteps on the stairs and the sound of the front door as it banged open hard enough to hit the wall behind it. Juniper pelted downstairs, slipping halfway down and bumping the rest of the way on her back. She scrambled up and slammed the door shut, turned the deadbolt, then hurried back up to her room and pulled the curtains aside. She opened the window and leaned out just in time to see a dark figure vanish into the tall rows of wheat.

"Junie?"

• 12 •

SHE DIDN'T MOVE, so Laura said it again: "Junie? Are you okay, honey?"

She flicked on the bedroom light and blinked, taking in the mess. The floor was littered with clothes, the mattress askew on the bed.

"There was somebody in the house," Juniper said. "Watching me." Juniper's voice was flat. She clearly didn't expect Laura to believe her. But the last thing Laura wanted was another argument.

"Are you sure you weren't having a bad dream?"

"I know when I'm dreaming and when I'm awake. Whoever it was, they ran away."

Laura went to the window and stood beside her daughter, looking out across the yard. The wheat, the barn, the distant trees, and the smell of the sea. Nothing like Blue Valley.

"They were in the house?" she said.

"You sound like you totally believe me."

"I don't *dis*believe you. How about that, Junie? I definitely heard a lot of noise."

"There was an eye in the closet, and I poked it, and then an octopus came out and tried to get me, but I smashed it and it ran away."

"I see."

"Okay," Juniper said. "I know it sounds insane. I get it. But come here."

She crossed the room to the closet. The door was ajar and Juniper opened it the rest of the way. The rack of clothes was parted in the middle. Juniper stepped inside the shallow space and pointed at the wall. "See? There's a hole."

Laura went and stood beside her. There was indeed a hole, roughly three inches in diameter, four feet up from the floor.

"You're saying somebody was peeping in at you?"

Juniper nodded.

"You're saying someone was in the house," Laura said.

"That's exactly what I'm saying."

Laura left the room and walked down the hall to the linen closet. Juniper followed. Laura reached up and pulled the chain attached to the bare bulb overhead. She remembered removing the towels and sheets from the shelves, and now she wondered why she hadn't seen the hole before.

She bent and looked through into Juniper's room, saw the clothes and the closet door frame and beyond it the bed. Past that she could see the window. A slice of Charlotte Jessen's old bedroom was clearly visible from inside the linen closet.

"Now do you believe me?"

Laura looked around at the bare white walls and the empty shelves. She ran her finger through a smear of leftover dust and smiled.

"Look," she said. She pointed at the dry husk of a dead moth. "We didn't do a very good job cleaning up. This closet was full of moths."

"So?"

"So, do you think maybe, in the dark—"

"You think I saw some moths flying out of a hole in my wall and thought they were tentacles?"

"Well, it was dark. And this is—"

"Right. A tiny moth is the same thing as a huge squid. Totally the same."

"Come on, Juniper. Which thing makes the most sense?"

"You know what? Fine. I know it sounds crazy. I *told* you it sounded crazy."

"All I'm saying—"

Laura cut herself off and closed her eyes. She had been trying so hard to avoid an argument, but here they were. The destination was inevitable; it was only the journey that changed.

When Juniper spoke again her voice was softer. She sounded sad and hurt. "I'm sorry. There's no way an octopus creature was creeping on me in Grandma's closet. I get it."

Laura breathed a sigh of relief. She opened her eyes and reached out. Juniper allowed herself to be pulled into a sideways hug, her sharp hip poking into Laura's thigh.

"When I was a kid I used to have night terrors," Laura said. "You know what those are?"

"Like nightmares where you think you're awake?"

"Kind of like that, yeah. They were scary and they felt real to me. I'm not saying you didn't see anything. I'm just saying maybe your brain was half asleep and it was processing things weird. Isn't that possible?"

"I guess. But it seemed legit to me."

"I bet it did. You wanna switch rooms with me?"

"No, thanks. I'm not giving up the big room that easy."

Laura walked Juniper back to her room and got her back into bed. She untangled the sheet and shook it out, letting it drift gently down over Juniper's body. She shut the closet door.

"Sleep tight," she said. "If anything else happens, holler for me, okay? I'll leave my door open."

"Would you close my door?"

"Don't you want to leave it open?"

"I'd rather have it closed."

Laura sighed again but didn't argue. She turned off the light and stepped into the hall. She took a last look at her daughter before she shut the door.

• 13 •

J UNIPER CREPT OUT of bed and put her ear to the door, listened for the sound of Laura retreating down the hall to her own room. Her mother had grown up in the yellow farmhouse; the room she was sleeping in had always been hers. But Juniper's room was new to her and it would take some time to get used to it. She was still struggling with the idea that they would never return to Blue Valley, and was trying to figure out how to bring the subject up without admitting she had eavesdropped.

When she was certain her mother was in bed, Juniper turned on the light. She checked the bedroom closet again to make sure she was alone and looked through the hole into the empty linen closet. No strangers in there, no monsters or moths. Just a dark, empty compartment.

She went to the window. Moonlight glazed the tops of wheat stalks and cast long shadows from the barn. An owl flew from one tree to another, something limp dangling from its talons. But she didn't see anything watching the house. She felt sure she had injured the creature in the closet. Maybe she had hurt it enough that it would never come back. She closed the window and pulled the curtains.

She missed her father. Missed him so much that she felt empty, like she would never be a whole human being again. He would have believed her. He would have searched the house and the grounds, looked under her bed and tucked her in. And she would have felt safe.

There was a separate compartment built into the lid of her suitcase and Juniper unzipped it, reached in, and pulled out a handful of mementos—things she had not been able to leave behind, even for the week she thought she'd be gone. Her most cherished treasure was a strip of three black and white photos, dispensed by a booth at a pizza place when she was five.

She had hundreds of photos of her father stored on her phone or in the cloud, but the curled band of photographic paper was the only physical reminder of him she had brought with her. In the pictures they were both mugging for the camera, making silly faces, and she remembered how his beard had tickled her cheek as they huddled in close to get in the camera's field of vision. It no longer made her cry to look at him, but her throat still closed up.

She flopped back onto the bed and stared at him, at the two of them together. It was hard to imagine being as happy as the little girl in the pictures looked. It was hard to reconcile the young man her father had been with the gray-haired, middle-aged man he had become in the decade that separated the trip to the pizza place from his death. He had aged so quickly, and she knew she had contributed to that process. She had not always been the best daughter.

She rolled over and reached under the edge of the mattress. Her hand brushed against the folded page that she had cut from her grandmother's book. She pulled it out and opened it, smoothing it against her thigh.

She had never given her grandmother a lot of thought. She had met her a few times when she was little, and Charlotte Jessen had seemed like a nice old lady, but from an alien place and a much different time. The photo of the young man with Charlotte and the bizarre poem in her journal—or spell, or whatever it was—shifted the idea of her in Juniper's mind. She suspected her grandmother had been involved in a weird sex thing or a cult, which made her seem vastly more interesting. How eccentric had Charlotte Jessen been? Did her mother have any idea?

The first stanza of the spell-poem was different from the rest and seemed more like instructions than anything else. She read it out loud, keeping her voice low. She didn't want her mother bursting in on her again.

"An offering must be made," she read. "The loved one (a likeness in flames). Blood (become ashes). A contribution (from the field)." Two phrases, "in flames" and "become ashes," made Juniper think something had to be burned. "A loved one." But not an actual person—a "likeness." So maybe the little cornhusk doll that she'd found in the box, or maybe a photograph, like the one of the bare-chested young man who looked so much like Charlotte's dead husband. Was he a loved one?

Juniper started to think of the journal passage as an incantation, and the mention of blood made her pulse quicken. It added a layer of strangeness and an element of danger. The biggest mystery, though, was the reference to a "contribution from the field." The wheat field?

What kind of contribution?

Spurred by a sudden flash of inspiration, Juniper upended the trash can next to the bed and laid on her stomach so she could reach down and sort through its contents. Among the used tissues she found the remains of the cutworm. It wasn't a stalk of wheat, but it was most definitely from the field.

She realized that she was starting to take the incantation seriously. She also understood that she needed something to keep herself occupied. If she was indeed hallucinating tentacles in the closet, she must be incredibly stressed. And if there were actual tentacles in the closet, it might be best not to think too hard about them.

She hesitated for a moment and—not entirely sure what she was doing or why she was doing it—she tore a picture of her father from the photo booth strip and dropped it into the empty trash can. Her father looked up at her from the bottom of the bin, grinning, eyes crossed, tongue sticking out. Her chest tightened.

She closed her eyes and dropped the worm's tiny body onto her father's face, then retrieved her razor blade from under the lamp. She drew the blade across her left index finger, watched it bite into her flesh, and closed her eyes. She squeezed until she heard a drop plunk against the bottom of the trash can and then pressed a used tissue against the wound.

Apparently the next step—if she was really going to continue doing this—was to burn it all. She found the matches under her mattress and almost dropped them trying to spark one to life. She managed to get a flame going and dropped the lit match in the trash can. She watched, fascinated, as the other items caught fire, the worm's body crackling as it burned, the cheap paper photograph of her father curling at one edge, then browning and turning to ash. She was worried about smoke, worried her mother might smell it and wake up, but there wasn't enough fuel for the fire to grow. It petered out in seconds, leaving a gunky residue in the bottom of the can.

"That's it?" Juniper said. She wasn't sure what she had expected. Still, it was pointless to leave the task half finished. She picked up the piece of paper covered with her grandmother's handwriting—at least, she assumed it was Charlotte's—and took a deep breath before reciting the lines.

"From this likeness, with this blood, I accept the burden. From this petitioner, with this tribute, I accept the sorrow. From love, with agony, I wait."

What burden? What agony? Wait for what?

She checked the trash can. It was unchanged. She went to the closet and looked through the hole again. The linen closet was still empty.

Maybe I have to read the Danish parts.

So she did, struggling with the pronunciation. She read it again, in case she had mangled something, then folded the paper and slipped it back under her mattress. She sat cross-legged on her bed and peeked under the tissue wrapped around her finger. The cut wasn't bleeding, so she chucked the tissue in the trash can and picked the other tissues up off the floor, tossing them in, too. They barely covered the bottom of the bin, hiding the black stain of burnt worm and paper.

She got into bed and pulled the thin sheet up to her chin and stared at the ceiling, feeling foolish and disappointed. Warm tears ran down her cheeks and along the curve of her throat, making her skin itch. Time passed and she eventually fell asleep.

• 14 •

L AURA WOKE UP to bright sunlight streaming through her window and across her face. She rubbed her eyes and looked around her childhood bedroom at the posters of Kylie Minogue and *Betty Blue*, the rack of cassette tapes, and the vanity mirror plastered with fading photographs of Thomas Helmig and David Bowie. She had spent hours and days and years in that room, nursing small dramas and big dreams. Coming home after so long, she had expected to feel like a child again, but her mother wasn't there to wake her up and make her breakfast. Laura felt very old and tired.

She got out of bed and went to the tiny bathroom to brush her teeth. On her way back to her room she checked in on her daughter. Juniper was curled up in the big bed, the duvet wrapped around her head. There was a faint whiff of smoke in the air and Laura wondered which of their faraway neighbors was burning leaves.

She dressed quickly and was leaving her room when she noticed the miniature chest the lawyer had given her, Charlotte's bequest to them. She hadn't looked closely at it before, and now she saw the latch was broken. She lifted the lid and looked inside, disappointed to see a haphazard collection of junk, an old woman's miscellany drawer. She paged through the leather-bound grimoire but saw nothing that would cast light on her mother's life. At the bottom of the box was an old photograph of her parents, and she took it, slipping it into her pocket before going downstairs to the kitchen.

She was trying to decide between leftover pork and potatoes or pickled fish with crackers when she was startled by a knock at the back door. Anders stood on the stone terrace, leaning on his crutches, a knapsack slung over one shoulder. He grinned at her.

"Hope I didn't wake you," he said.

"Come in," Laura said. "I was just trying to figure out breakfast, but I think I'm gonna have to run into town."

"How long since you've had aebleskiver?"

He clomped past her into the kitchen, propped the crutches against the counter and opened his knapsack, producing a carton of eggs, a quart of milk, a pint of fresh butter, a jar of strawberry jam, and a cotton bag that puffed out a cloud of flour when he plopped it down on the counter.

"Dammit, I forgot the sugar," he said. "But the eggs are fresh from my farm. And so's the flour."

Laura went to the cupboard over the stove and stood on her toes, peering into the shadows. She pushed aside a box of rat poison and found a small bag of sugar at the back of the bottom shelf. She turned around and presented it to Anders like a trophy.

"We're in luck," she said. "Actual ingredients are an endangered species around here."

"I ran into Anna in town last night and she told me you hadn't bought any groceries yet. Sounded like you had dinner well in hand, but I thought you might be hungry this morning."

"You're a life saver. You didn't bring your boy?"

"Magnus? I imagine he's out in the field somewhere. He was already gone before I woke up."

With Anders's help, Laura found a set of mixing bowls,

a spatula, and a stained black aebleskiver pan with individual holes for the little cakes. They were pleasantly surprised to find a spice rack on the back of the pantry door, along with an ancient bottle of vegetable oil that somehow wasn't rancid. Anders whisked ingredients while Laura heated the oil. Anders limped over with the bowl and dropped dollops of batter into the pan. They stood and watched the cakes brown, then Laura flipped them over. She added the jam and more batter.

"Kind of like old times, right?" Anders said.

"When did we ever cook together?"

"I mean being here, you and me."

"Anders, I hope you don't think . . ."

"I'm being neighborly, that's all," he said. "Don't worry. You're not the only one who's been through things." He leaned back against the counter and flashed her a sad smile. "It's just nice to see you again, Laura Loaf."

"Your wife . . ." Laura said.

"I don't think you ever knew her. She's not in the picture, though, if that's what you . . ." He trailed off and busied himself wiping the counter.

Laura shook her head, swiping a cloth at a clot of bright red jam that had oozed out over the rim of the pan.

"I don't think these are supposed to leak," she said.

"They'll taste fine."

"What happened to her—your wife?"

Anders sighed and rinsed out the dishcloth he was using, then draped it over the faucet to dry. "We lost a child a couple years ago," he said. "It was rough on her. On both of us, but she took it . . . I mean, she spent all her time in his room, stopped talking to me, and then one morning she was gone. No note or anything. Just packed a bag and left."

"So it's just you and Magnus now?"

"You know how it is."

Laura knew exactly how it was. She put her hand on his

arm but was afraid to do more than that. She thought if she hugged him he might misunderstand the gesture, and she worried she might cry.

"Gross," Juniper said.

She was standing under the arch wearing the same clothes as the previous day, but there was a fresh green streak in her hair. Laura took a step away from Anders, who smiled at Juniper and twirled a spoon at her.

"We're making a special Danish breakfast," he said. "Ever had *aebleskiver* before?"

Juniper shook her head.

"How many you want?"

"Zero," Juniper said. "You guys can make out if you want. I'm gonna see if there's anything to do in town. My expectations are pretty low."

"Junie, honey," Laura began, but Juniper was already gone, the kitchen door banging shut behind her.

"I'm sorry," Laura said to Anders. "It's not you."

"Don't worry," he said. "They all go through a phase like this."

Laura shook her head. "Juniper's different."

"Well, she's American. I have no idea how that changes things for her. Or for you."

Laura frowned at him. "I think the aebleskiver's burning," she said.

"Oh, crap."

Laura got two plates and popped the crispy cakes out of the pan. Slathered with more strawberry jam they tasted fine. The two of them sat at the little table in the kitchen and ate in silence.

Laura finally pushed her plate away and sighed. "I can't eat them all," she said.

"You didn't even try."

"They're good, though. I should save the rest for Juniper."

"I'll leave the flour and eggs," Anders said. "You can make more for her."

"Maybe I won't burn them."

Laura remembered the photograph in her pocket and pulled it out, set it on the table where she could see it. "She would have burned them, too," she said. "She was such a terrible cook. Even her coffee was bad, but she still got up and made a pot every morning."

"I know," Anders said. "My stomach hurts just thinking about her coffee."

"You said you helped her out around here?"

"When I could."

"Were you there when she . . ."

"I was on the tractor. I heard her and came running, but it was too late. Tor wasn't the same after we brought in the corn." He sighed. "But she loved him, you know."

"He was still here when you found her?" Laura looked around the kitchen, trying to imagine her mother's final moments, but the homemade yellow curtains and the cozy round table reminded her of childhood and comfort and safety. It was impossible to picture her parents as they must have been near the end. She shuddered. "Did he fight you?"

"Like a tiger," Anders said.

"That's how that happened?" Laura gestured at the plaster cast on Anders's leg and he rapped on it with his knuckles.

"Lucky all he broke was my leg," he said.

"Wait," Laura said. "I wasn't paying attention. You said this flour was from your farm?"

"Harvest was a few days ago."

"But what about Magnus?"

Anders shook his head and pointed at the kitchen door. "Magnus didn't come from my fields, he came from yours."

75

• 15 •

J UNIPER WALKED to the tree line and stopped, unable to see a way through the underbrush and unwilling to wade into the dense green. Despite what she had told her mother, she had no real desire to spend time in the village. There were no interesting shops, no movie theaters, no bookstores. Only a handful of small businesses. She couldn't imagine what people in Godhavn did for fun.

Exploring the woods sounded vaguely appealing, but that looked impossible.

She started walking again and veered to her left, toward the waving fields of wheat and the inevitable path into town. She had forgotten a jacket and the air was chilly, but she didn't want to return to the house. She didn't like Anders. She understood that Laura might feel lonely, but you were *supposed* to feel lonely after your husband died. You were supposed to grieve, and it ought to take a long time. What you were not supposed to do was move halfway around the world, ruin your daughter's life, and flirt with old boyfriends.

The path to town was not paved, and the dirt was cushioned with dead leaves and wheat chaff, lending her step a spring she didn't feel. She put out her hand and swept it across the resilient stalks as she walked, relishing the tingle in her fingertips, then stopped and grabbed a handful of them, intending to pull the plants out by the root. But she couldn't bring herself to damage them. She let go and patted the air in front of the row in an apologetic gesture, worried she had upset the crop.

On a whim, she left the path and walked into the field, letting the wheat close in behind her, willing to get lost and daydreaming that she might never be found. She immediately felt at peace, cocooned in the rustling plants and the soft whisper of the wind. She raised her face to the sun and drifted farther away from the path, deeper into the golden field. She felt buoyant, like a cork on the surface of a vast ocean, the crops drawing her along and lifting her up.

A hissing sound woke her from her reverie, and she turned to see someone watching her from behind the nearest row—a single eye visible through the wheat.

"Hey," she said.

The eye disappeared and Juniper heard footsteps as the spy scampered away. She pushed through the rows and followed, running now, despite the resistance of the wheat, tripping over ruts, bending and breaking stalks. They sprang back at her, scratching her arms and neck, but she kept her eyes on the tassels above, watching for the telltale quiver of someone moving through the field.

She was concentrating so hard on the person ahead that she didn't notice the ground sloping upward until she came out in a clearing at the top of a high hill.

Magnus stood waiting, panting softly and grinning at her. There was gauze taped over his left eye.

When she had caught her breath, Juniper pointed at him. "It was you last night! I saw you run away!"

Magnus shrugged.

"How'd you get in my house?"

He shrugged again.

"Does it hurt? Your eye? Did I poke it all the way out?"

Magnus reached up and pulled at the tape, lifting the gauze. Something bulged and rippled in the shadows where

his eye should have been. A glossy tendril flicked out at her. She backed away to where the wheat bordered the clearing, and Magnus smoothed the bandage back into place.

"What the fuck was that? What are you?" She was ready to turn and run back into the dense rows, but curiosity rooted her to the spot.

Magnus put a finger to his lips, then pointed at the field below. Juniper looked and saw a man standing far enough away that she had to squint. He was shirtless, and when the wind moved through the wheat, she caught a glimpse of his bare, pink thigh.

"He's naked," she said.

Magnus giggled.

Something about the man, his posture (the way he squared his shoulders, his head cocked to one side) or his thin hair (the color of the surrounding wheat, blowing gently in the breeze) reminded her of someone. Then he turned his head and looked directly at her, and she fell backward, scrambling away from the clearing. She rolled over and got her feet under her and ran. She didn't know where the path was—or the house or the town—and she didn't care.

The man in the field looked exactly like her dead father.

• 16 •

LAURA WAS WASHING the aebleskiver pan when Juniper
burst in through the kitchen door, ran through the
arch and scrambled up the stairs. Laura dried her hands and
followed, pausing at the bottom of the stairs to listen before
going up. The door to Juniper's room was closed and Laura
knocked. When there was no answer, she took a deep breath
and opened it.

Juniper was sitting on the edge of the bed, her hands
clamped between her knees. She didn't immediately yell at
her mother for invading her privacy, which let Laura know
that whatever had happened was serious. She stepped over
the crumpled black suit that Juniper still hadn't put away, sat
down next to her and rubbed her back. Juniper leaned against
her and put her head on Laura's shoulder.

"What happened, Junie?"

Juniper shook her head. Laura held her and waited. After
a few minutes Juniper sat up straight and wiped her eyes, but
she didn't pull away.

"I think I'm going crazy," Juniper said. Her voice was soft
and punctuated by hiccups. "I saw Dad."

"Oh, honey," Laura said.

"I know. I'm so stupid. And it was totally weird."

"When you miss somebody—"

"I know, I know. But this wasn't like a dream or something.

It was just now, in the daytime, and he was naked, Mom. He was standing in the middle of the wheat and he wasn't wearing any clothes. Why would I imagine Dad naked?" Juniper finally pulled away. She stood up and grabbed the box of tissues from the table.

"You saw your dad in the field?" Laura said carefully. "In *our* field?"

"Well, I thought I did. Because my stupid brain is obviously melting." Juniper tossed a tissue at the trash can and missed. Laura bent and picked it up.

"Your brain isn't melting," she said.

She dropped the tissue in the can and a puff of ashes rose up and settled back down.

Laura tipped the can toward her and shook the tissues to one side. There was a shiny black residue at the bottom. "Did you burn something in here?" She watched Juniper glance at the trash can, saw the guarded look return to her daughter's eyes, and she knew. "Junie?"

"Oh," Juniper said. "That was just . . . I don't know. I was goofing around."

"Juniper, what did you do?"

"Who cares? Didn't you hear me? I'm going crazy. So what if I burned some paper?"

Laura's stomach clenched and for a moment she thought she might throw up. Her face felt hot, and she had a curious sensation of being far away from her own body.

"What did you burn? What paper?"

Juniper's face went blank and she stared down at the floor, her arms crossed.

"You can tell me," Laura said. "What was it?"

"It was hardly anything at all, and it burned out right away and I won't do it again."

"Was it a picture of your dad?"

"It wasn't what you think. I wasn't mad or lashing out or anything like that. I was just bored."

Laura examined the inside of the trash can and counted to ten in her head. She needed to remain calm. At last she stood and pointed to the suit on the floor. "Pick that up and shake it out. Your dad's gonna need some clothes."

"You believe me?"

Laura nodded. "I believe you."

Juniper surprised her by giving her a hug. Laura squeezed her back, then pulled away and held Juniper at arm's length, frowning down at her. "Junie?" she said. "Did you cut yourself?"

"What?"

"You must have."

"Well," Juniper said. "Yeah, but just my finger. Not like before."

"What did you use?"

Juniper tipped the table lamp and slid a razor blade from beneath its base. Laura slid it the rest of the way across the table so she could pick it up. She held it carefully between her finger and her thumb and turned it in the light. There was a black smear on one side.

"Let me see it."

Juniper held out her index finger without protest. There was a nearly invisible cut on the pad, already nearly healed.

"Who told you to do this? Was it Magnus? What else did he say?"

"Nobody told me," Juniper said. "It was in Grandma's diary. I'm sorry I cut myself. I know I promised, but—"

"What diary?"

Juniper knelt and slipped her hand under the mattress, pulled out a folded piece of paper, and handed it to her mother.

"It was in that box of junk."

Laura smoothed the paper out and read the familiar instructions in her mother's unsteady handwriting. She had known the words by heart since childhood.

"You went through with this?" she said. "What was your offering from the field?"

"A worm."

"A worm?"

"It was already dead."

"But a worm isn't . . ." Laura sighed. "Juniper, with patience and hard work, the crops come back every year. That's what this place is all about. The wheat? The peas and corn? In a way, they're all part of the land. But a worm . . . that's just flesh. It comes and goes."

"I didn't know."

Laura stood up and folded the paper again, shoving it into the pocket of her jeans.

"Okay," she said. "What's done is done, but you brought him here, so you have to take care of him. That's how this works."

"So Dad's really back?"

"In a sense. Come on. Get the suit and let's go."

• 17 •

SHE WAS AFRAID she wouldn't be able to find the hilltop again. They got turned around twice and had to backtrack, but finally Juniper felt the ground sloping upward, and they emerged from the wheat with a clear view of the entire farm. Juniper pointed to the spot where she had seen her father, but he was gone. Nor was there any sign of Magnus.

"He was right there," she said. "I swear."

"I believe you, Junie."

Laura shaded her eyes and scanned the horizon.

"There," she said. "There he is."

Juniper looked and saw movement near the house. She squinted and saw it was her father, tugging at the barn door, ratcheting it open along its track.

"Is he trying to hide?"

"He's bonded to this field. He's probably looking for tools to take care of it."

They held hands and hurried back through the field, this time on a straight path toward the house, the barn, and the tree line that bordered the dense, dark woods. Her grandfather's suit, draped over her mother's shoulder, rippled in the breeze as they ran. The wheat whipped at them and slapped at their arms and thighs until they were finally through it and pounding across tall grass.

The hulder heard them and stopped yanking at the door. He turned and watched them and waited. When they drew near the circle of charred earth, he smiled and held out his arms.

He looked like Jacob Roux, but he was still naked. Juniper turned away, let go of her mother's hand and watched a grasshopper jump back and forth between two stalks of wheat. When she turned back around, he was dressed, and her mother was knotting the tie around his neck.

"There," Laura said. "Look how handsome he is."

She had barely finished her sentence when the tears came. She covered her face and sank to her knees. Juniper stood rooted, horrified, and unsure of what to do, but the hulder knelt down beside Laura and put his arm around her shoulders. She leaned into him, sobbing against his chest. He looked up at Juniper and smiled again, and for a moment Juniper could accept the illusion that her father was alive and that her parents were together.

Tor Jessen's suit didn't quite fit. It was tight across the shoulders. The jacket sleeves and trouser legs were too short, and the white shirt gapped between the buttons.

Tor had been a smaller man than Jacob Roux.

But Juniper smiled back at the hulder, and when he held out his hand she went to him, kneeled in the dirt and put her arms around her mother. Jacob wrapped his free arm around her, and she finally felt whole.

She knew it wasn't real, but in the moment it felt real enough, and when the tears came, she didn't hold them back.

• 18 •

INSIDE THE BARN was hot and dry, and dust motes tickled Juniper's nose. She sneezed and waved her hand in front of her face, which excited the motes and made her sneeze again.

There was an old car parked in the middle of the floor, rusted and sagging forward on two flat tires. Jacob gave it a wide berth as he examined the farming implements that were hung neatly on pegs along the south wall. He grabbed two scythes and held them out to Juniper. She chose one that had extra tines attached behind the blade, and they left the barn.

There was a cool breeze that tousled the tops of the trees and chilled the sweat on Juniper's forehead. Laura sat on the porch steps, watching them with an odd expression.

"Why does this one have more sickles on it?" Juniper said.

"It's not a sickle, it's a scythe," Laura said.

"I know that," Juniper said, though she had not known there was a difference. "But what's up with the extra blades?"

"It's called a grain cradle," Laura said. "It makes it easier to gather the wheat after you harvest it."

"Dad's scythe doesn't have a cradle."

"He's going to have a harder time bundling everything up when he's done," Laura said.

Juniper looked at her father and he shrugged. "I guess he doesn't care," Juniper said.

She followed him out to the field and watched as he lowered the end of his scythe to the ground, moving it in smooth arcs away from his body, shifting his weight from one leg to the other as the wheat fell behind him in waves. Juniper dragged her scythe to the next row and tried to mimic Jacob's motions, but the tool was heavy and she kept turning it, digging it into the soil and bouncing the cradle back toward her. She thought a lawn mower would be more effective. Eventually she laid the scythe down and crashed through the wheat to where her father was working. She walked behind him, marveling at how confident he was, how he seemed to know what he was doing.

"Did you used to live on a farm?"

He stopped and smiled at her, cocking his head to the side.

"I mean, I just realized I don't know if you ever did. Grandma Roux lived in that little apartment, but there's no way she lived there when you were a kid. There must be farms all around Blue Valley."

Jacob put his scythe down and sat on a pile of new mown wheat, crossing his legs in front of him. Juniper sat down beside him and picked up a stalk. She stuck it between her teeth and grinned.

"Now I fit in around here," she said. "See?"

But Jacob didn't smile, and Juniper felt foolish and sad and confused. She had missed her father, had grieved for him, and she still re-lived his death every night when she closed her eyes. She had wished for a chance to spend more time with him, but now that her wish had come true, she didn't know what to do with the pain. It hadn't disappeared when he came back.

They sat for a while, watching as the sun moved across the sky and shadows crept through the crops. When Juniper grew tired of listening to the crickets, she cleared her throat and said what she had been thinking. "You should have let me practice more in the parking lot, Dad."

Jacob looked at her, his face placid and unlined. He seemed younger than she remembered, as if he had stopped worrying about the things fathers worried about.

"If you listened to me, we wouldn't have been on the road when the deer was there, and right now I'd be home with you eating spaghetti and watching TV. Or maybe you would have come with us when Charlotte died and you'd still be here, but you'd be talking to me. Why don't you talk?"

Jacob looked away, and she knew he wanted to pick up the scythe and get back to work.

"If you could talk, you could tell me where you grew up and whether you lived on a farm or in a city somewhere. You could tell me about the house where you grew up. Maybe you lived there your whole life until you met Mom. Why don't I already know that? I probably should have asked when you were alive, huh?"

She felt her throat closing up, and her vision blurred. Jacob reached out, and Juniper grabbed his hand. It was the same as it ever was: the calluses, the thick boney knuckles, and the half-moon scar on his ring finger. She held her hand up to his, palm to palm, and suddenly felt small and safe, the way she had as a toddler when she had curled up in his lap. She turned her head away and blinked rapidly, willing the sudden tears to evaporate unseen, but it didn't work. She cried quietly this time, and Jacob sat next to her mutely. When, after a time, her eyes cleared, she could see out across the field to where Laura sat waiting for them, a tiny speck on the porch of the yellow house.

Juniper let go of Jacob's hand and wiped her nose on her forearm. She glanced at her father and flinched when his hand darted out at her. She felt a pinprick of pain, and then Jacob held up a wriggling cutworm.

"That was on me?" Juniper said. "Gross!"

Jacob squeezed the worm and black ichor squirted out across his fingers, followed by a drop of thick clear liquid. He dropped the tiny body in the dirt and wiped his hand on Tor Jessen's white shirt, then stood and picked up the scythe.

"Okay," Juniper said. She jumped up and brushed off the seat of her jeans. "If it's all right, I'll just help you. That cradle thing gets in the way."

Jacob lowered the blade and began the smooth mowing motion again. Juniper took a second to step on the dead worm, grinding it under her toes, then took the stalk of wheat from between her teeth and tossed it up in the air. She watched as the breeze grabbed it and carried it away over the tall tassels until she couldn't see it anymore.

• 19 •

JACOB SPENT all afternoon in the field, head down, arms swinging the scythe back and forth. Juniper returned to the barn and found a sickle, which she used to gather the wheat as he mowed it down, carrying it back to the flat grass and bundling it in sheaves. It felt weirdly normal to be working the field with her dad.

Finally she grew tired and went and sat on the porch next to her mother. Laura handed her a cup of lukewarm tea and she held it as she watched her father work. He was tireless, tramping along in the perfectly straight lines he created with the scythe.

"It's too weird," she said at last. "It's Dad, and it's not Dad. I don't know how to feel or what to do."

"Maybe just try to enjoy this extra time with him," Laura said.

"How long?"

Laura didn't respond, just took her hand, and Juniper let her. After a while Laura went inside, reheated their tea and came back out. They sat in companionable silence as Jacob worked, his scythe sweeping back and forth with clocklike regularity. When a vehicle crunched up the driveway, he stopped and stood, leaning on the scythe until Anna emerged from her truck with more Tupperware containers. Anna glanced at him, then waved at Laura and Juniper with her free hand, and Jacob returned to his chore.

"I thought you might need more food," Anna said as she ascended the porch steps.

"Oh, thank you," Laura said. She pointed out at the wheat. "This happened and we kind of lost track of the day. I never got a chance to shop."

"I know," Anna said. "I talked to Noah at the market and he said he hasn't met you yet." She held out her home cooked meal like a prize, and Laura took it. Juniper could see through the translucent plastic more pork, more potatoes, more mushy peas.

"Yay," she said. "Danish food."

Laura took the dishes into the house and Anna waited with one foot on the porch steps, considering Juniper as if she were an interesting lab experiment.

"We haven't met," Anna said. "You may call me Mrs. Schmidt."

"And you may call me Ms. Roux," Juniper said. She offered her hand.

Anna stifled a laugh. "Well met, Ms. Roux. May I sit?"

Juniper shrugged and scooted to one side to make room. Anna sat and made a show of settling in, rotating her shoulders and stretching out her legs one at a time to adjust her jeans. She nodded at the field where Jacob had finished cutting down a row and was moving on to another.

"How do you feel about that?"

"I don't know. How am I supposed to feel?"

"I don't think there's a right way or a wrong way."

"What are they called?"

"Hulders," Anna said.

"Right," Juniper said. She paused, thinking about the tentacles in her closet. "Magnus is one, too."

"Yes. But this particular hulder is unusual," Anna said, watching Jacob's rhythmic movements. "The making of it."

"How so?"

The screen door banged open and Laura emerged from the house carrying another steaming mug. "Because your father wasn't born in Godhavn," she said. "I thought you might like some tea, Anna."

"Thank you," Anna said, accepting the cup. "But that wasn't—"

"Hulders originated here and it's kind of forbidden to make them in other places," Laura interrupted. "People grow up here and move away and sometimes they want to carry on the traditions, but—"

"But there are some traditions that we should keep to ourselves," Anna said. She shot a pointed look at Laura over the rim of her cup.

"I get it," Juniper said. "It's not that Dad wasn't from here. It's me. I wasn't born here. I'm not supposed to make hulders."

"No," Anna said. "No, you are not."

"It's done now," Laura said.

"He doesn't talk," Juniper said. "Neither does Magnus. Do any of them talk?"

"Most of them do," Anna said. "Magnus never talked. He was born strange. But creating a hulder is not an exact science. You never quite know what you'll get."

"Seems random. Why make them at all?"

"Hmm," Anna said. She glanced at Laura again, then took another sip of tea and cleared her throat. "Years ago, the *byrådet*—the town council—noticed that young people were going away, to university and to big cities, and they weren't coming back to Godhavn."

"I could have told you that would happen," Juniper said. "There's nothing to keep people here. I'd get away as fast as I could."

"This place has its charms," Laura said.

"It does," Anna said. "But this is a farming community,

and most kids don't want to be farmers anymore. There are more exciting opportunities in Copenhagen. And in America."

She raised an eyebrow at Laura, but Laura was staring out at the tree line. Juniper followed her mother's gaze and saw a family of deer cross through the shadows between two trees.

"Anyway," Anna said. "it was becoming a problem because there were fewer and fewer strong young people left to plant the fields or harvest the crops. Neighbors cooperated, helped each other when and where they could, but the community was dying. Until somebody remembered an old tradition and created a hulder to help with the farm. It worked, so the next year somebody else did it, and as more of us brought hulders in to help, Godhavn began to thrive again."

"So they're just farmers? That's why Dad suddenly knows how to mow down a field of wheat with something he found in the barn?"

"That was the original idea."

"Why doesn't he use a tractor?"

"Maybe because they're ancient creatures and they come from ancient traditions," Anna said.

"The real answer," Laura said, "is that nobody knows. They don't seem to understand complicated tools."

"But they are very focused on their tasks," Anna said. "Old Lucas Agard brings his grandfather and uncles back every season to work his farm. They knew what they were doing when they were alive, and they know it still."

"Magnus doesn't seem like he'd be a very good farmer," Juniper said.

"Farming is how it started," Laura said, "but when people realized they could bring back a sort of . . . I guess, a version of their loved ones, it turned into something else. It means different things to different people."

"Yes," Anna said. "Old Lucas wants someone to help him bring in his crops, but young Anders Karlsen wanted to spend one more season with his son, who died three years ago. It's as common now to create a hulder for sentimental reasons as it is to create one for business reasons."

"Mine is sentimental," Juniper said. "Even if I didn't know what I was doing."

"Yes," Anna said. She looked at Laura again.

"Wait," Juniper said. "You said he wanted to spend one more season with Magnus. What happens after the season?"

"Juniper," Laura said, "your tea's getting cold again. Why don't you go stick it in the microwave?"

"I don't even like tea. Just tell me."

"You should know," Anna said, "the hulder is made of four things."

"Blood and a picture and a bug or something," Juniper said. "That's three. What's the last thing?"

"Intent," Laura said. "You have to really want it."

"A bug?" Anna said. "No, it doesn't require a bug, it needs an offering from the field. A blade of grass or a stalk of wheat or a kernel of corn. It doesn't have to be much, but it must come from the earth because that's what binds it to this place."

"Pretty creepy."

"And once the harvest comes in, the contract is fulfilled, and the bond is broken."

"And it disappears," Juniper said. "That makes sense, I guess."

"No," Laura said. "It doesn't disappear."

"It turns on the one who created it," Anna said. "And sometimes it turns on other people it encounters. It needs a purpose or it becomes confused and angry. A hulder cannot be allowed to exist beyond a single season. This is why it must be destroyed as soon as the crops come in."

Far out over the sea of wheat, Jacob's head popped up. He grinned at them and waved.

Juniper hesitated a second before waving back.

• 20 •

THEY WALKED through the grass, a wide swath of it that curved between the dried stubs of harvested corn and the wild woods, until they came to a narrow path that led away from the farm.

Laura stopped and picked a handful of wildflowers: poppies and horsetails and tiny, colorful eyebrights. Jacob watched her, frowning, his forehead creased with concern. He was bonded to the land, and Juniper wondered if he felt protective of everything that grew there. She walked for a while between her parents, thinking she might shield her mother if the hulder was angry about the flowers, but Jacob was eventually distracted by a cutworm crawling up the slender trunk of a sapling. He plucked it off the tree and stuck it in his pocket.

They made their way through the woods, the sun angling low in the west, revealing unexpected colors along the path. They heard the tide first, then smelled the briny freshness of the water and came out of the woods at the edge of a little graveyard that overlooked the sea, bounded all around by a low, wrought-iron fence.

Jacob left them there and disappeared into the woods.

Laura watched him go, then entered the cemetery, stepping carefully on the wide stones that were laid between the plots. Juniper followed, aware that she was walking on the bodies of her ancestors. The graves near the fence were newer, marked with marble and granite, one or two decorated with brass plaques. Closer to the middle of the cemetery the head-stones were old and crumbling, and the names carved into them were unreadable.

The freshest grave was also the farthest from the water, with a pink granite stone:

CHARLOTTE JESSEN
LOVING WIFE AND MOTHER

Next to it was a matching headstone that had suffered some mild erosion:

TOR JESSEN
A GOOD PROVIDER

Laura divided the flowers she had picked, laying half of them on each grave, and stepped back with her hands folded. Juniper had never seen her mother pray before. It hadn't occurred to her that Laura might be religious, but she bowed her head and waited until her mother turned to leave.

"Where do you think Dad went?" she said.

"I don't know," Laura said. "We should have left him at the farm. They don't like to be reminded they have graves."

"He just came with us," Juniper said. "I didn't invite him."

"I know."

"Do you miss them? Charlotte and Tor?"

Laura nodded.

"I miss Dad."

"I know, Junie."

They walked out toward the sea, climbing over rocks until they had a good view of the water, the sun sinking into a rippling pool of red and orange, a faraway sailboat drifting on the waves. They found a boulder and sat. A gull swooped past them and settled on the water's surface, watching to see if they had anything to eat.

"Why do we . . . that lady said we have to destroy him. But he's totally harmless, except if you're a worm. I don't think he would hurt us."

"It's as much for them as it is for us, Junie. Do you remember our cat?"

"Buttermilk?"

"Your dad had Buttermilk when I met him. I have no idea how old that cat was."

"She was basically dust with fur on it. She hissed at me every time I tried to pet her."

"Yeah, she wasn't very sociable in her old age."

"What's Buttermilk got to do with Dad?"

"Buttermilk had cancer. So, we had to put her down. The vet gave her a shot and she went to sleep and didn't wake up."

"I know how it's done."

"Okay, well, it's sort of the same thing when you make a hulder. They have a lifespan, and it's better for everybody—including them—if you help them out at the end. It could be considered a mercy, I guess. Part of them is the person they look like, but part of them is something else, and that part isn't very . . . comfortable here. When the time comes—" Laura broke off, and they turned to watch Jacob, who had reappeared and was scrambling over the rocks toward them, the tail of his suit coat flapping in the breeze. His hands were cupped together, and when he got closer he opened them.

Cradled in his palm was a baby mouse, pink and bald, its eyes sealed shut. It squirmed and nuzzled at the base of Jacob's thumb. Its belly gaped open, and Juniper saw a tiny round nut stuffed under its ribcage. She screamed and knocked Jacob's hand away. The mouse bounced off a rock and splashed into a pool of trapped water near the shoreline.

Jacob stared after it. Laura reached past Juniper and

patted him on the shoulder. "Thank you, Jacob," she said. "That was a very thoughtful gift. I'm sure my parents would have liked it."

She pulled Juniper to her feet and they all made their way back to solid land. The sun was setting, the colors were fading, and the wind had picked up. They followed Jacob back to the path through the woods. Laura reached for Juniper's hand, but Juniper pulled it away.

"You told me Buttermilk ran away," she said.

• 21 •

KASPAR HENRIKSEN woke up on the floor of his bedroom feeling hollowed out. His scalp was too tight and his tongue was stuck to the roof of his mouth. It took him a long moment to remember Agnes on the pier, and everything after that was a blur of vodka and pain pills.

He stumbled to the bathroom and threw up, then brushed his teeth and drank three glasses of water. He stared at the big clock on the bathroom wall for a long minute, rocking back and forth on the balls of his feet, trying to focus his bleary eyes. He had slept through most of the day, a thing he had done only once before. Luckily he'd had no appointments and had missed nothing.

He found a bottle of aspirin, but it was empty, and he wondered if he had mistaken it for his bottle of pills the previous night. When he noticed the cut on his palm, it immediately started to hurt, which made no sense—it had not bothered him before he saw it. He cleaned it, and when it started bleeding again he used shaving plaster to seal the wound.

He threw up again, drank another glass of water and stumbled out of the bathroom, headed for the tiny kitchen. With a handful of crackers in his stomach, he went back to the bedroom and dressed in the clothes he had worn the day before. There was a new hole in the cuff of his best tweed jacket, but he had no plans to see anyone so he wore it anyway.

He walked along the water's edge to his office. The air had grown colder. A chill wind gusted up the back of his jacket and cleared his head. He felt suddenly hungry and thought about stopping in at the bakery next door for a pastry, but changed his mind when he saw that his office door was ajar.

He pushed it the rest of the way open and saw wet footprints across the battered wooden floor leading into darkness. He stepped inside and turned on the overhead lights.

Agnes sat behind the ancient, second-hand desk in the corner of the room. She was naked, her dripping red hair hanging down over her shoulders and breasts. Her hands were folded in front of her on the desk, and when she turned her head to look at him, he saw that she had lost her left eye. Something shifted behind the hole in her skull, and a much larger eye, its iris a color Henriksen had never seen before, peeked out from the ruined socket, blinked twice and disappeared back into the darkness.

"You don't look good," Agnes said.

"I drank too much last night," he said. "I was upset."

"You know you shouldn't drink."

"There was no one to scold me about it."

"You pushed me into the water."

"You were going to kill me."

"Yes."

This led to an awkward silence, and Henriksen took the opportunity to close the door and lock it. He wondered if the old women at the cafe had seen Agnes come naked over the seawall and through the alley to his office. If so, they would not expect him to open for business tomorrow.

Agnes rose and came around the side of the desk, watching him. He averted his eyes. He was a gentleman. "You're not wearing anything," he said. "It's not proper." He took off his tweed and held it out to her. She came forward, took it and covered herself. She was very close now, and he knew he

would be unable to reach the door before she leapt. But he had no intention of running. This was his office. This was his secretary.

"There should be more time," he said. "It's too early. I used chaff from Anders Karlsen's farm, and he hasn't destroyed the boy yet. If the boy is still—"

"The boy is from another field," Agnes said. "And Farmer Karlsen has not yet caught him. But I am tired. This is the fifth time you've made me. Agnes is not so young anymore."

"You have always been young in my eyes," he said. "And so beautiful." His voice was barely a whisper, and the words he spoke surprised him. He had never said them out loud before.

"You have been kind to us," she said. "But we will not endure a sixth season in this skin."

"I understand," Henriksen said. "But please, could you not look like her when you do it? I do not want to see her that way."

She seemed confused by the request, and he thought he might need to repeat it, but she finally nodded and reached up, used her fingernails to rip the Agnes face away and reveal the black writhing things beneath it.

Henriksen screamed.

"Is this better?" the Agnes hulder said. When it spoke now, its word overlapped and grated against each other like rusty gears.

He nodded. "I only wanted to be near you a little longer," he said. "*Jeg har altid elsket dig.*"

The Agnes hulder nodded.

"Perhaps you did love her," it said. "But it might have been better to find someone who loved you back." It threw the jacket to the ground and leapt at him. The last thing Kaspar Henriksen saw was a drop of blood soaking into the collar of his favorite tweed.

I'll never wear that again, he thought.

• 22 •

SHE WAS DREAMING again.

She held the razor blade, gripped tight between her finger and thumb, and she pushed it into her flesh, forcing it past the surface and down into the meat. She stared—fascinated, as if watching a documentary about animal behavior—as the blade moved down the length of her forearm, a full third of it embedded in her.

But there was no blood. That's how she knew it was a dream.

Black ichor oozed out, thick and slow. She removed the blade from her arm and threw it in the trash can next to the bed. Already her skin was healing, knitting itself up along the path of the laceration like a train steaming down its track. Far from comforting her, the gradual absence of injury made her angry. She poked her pinkie finger into the last quarter inch of open wound and wiggled it around, determined to create as much damage as possible.

But it didn't hurt. That's how she knew it was a dream.

She pulled her finger out and watched, bemused, as clumps of dirt tumbled out along the curve of her arm and onto the bed. Something was visible down inside the cut, and she used her fingernails to pull out a leaf, shyly curled around itself, thin and papery and spotted with brown.

She stared at it for a moment, then dropped it into the trash can where it drifted down atop the razor blade.

When she looked at her arm again there was no wound.

She woke and looked at the clock on the table beside the lamp. It was nearly two-thirty. She rubbed her eyes and examined her perfect, healthy arm, then rose and went to the window.

Her father was on the lawn below, crouched low to the ground. He sensed her watching him and stood, looking up at her window. He was shirtless, holding a long-handled knife, his chest smeared with dark blood. A deer thrashed about at his feet, turning in wide circles on the grass, intestines trailing behind it.

The hulder smiled and waved.

Juniper sat on the bed and pulled her shoes on, then crept out of her room and down the stairs. The kitchen was dark and still. Juniper eased open the back door and shut it carefully behind her. It was brighter outside than it had been in the house and she opened her arms wide, welcoming the fresh, cool night air. The horizon glowed with orange bonfires and smoke drifted above distant fields. Her father was waiting for her, and when she approached he handed her the sickle she had used earlier in the day.

Juniper looked down at the doe. She was panicked, her eyes huge and dark, her hide wet, blood spouting in a regular rhythm from her abdomen. When Juniper reached out the doe tried to get up, but her strength gave out, and she fell back onto the grass.

"I saw this in the woods today," Juniper said. "When Anna was here. It was grazing there behind the trees."

He cocked his head to the side. She wasn't sure whether he understood what she was saying.

"How did you catch it? Why are you killing it?"

As if in answer, he knelt beside the deer and drew his blade across its throat. It bellowed in pain and thrashed again.

A rear hoof struck him in the arm, and Juniper heard a sickening crunch. Juniper watched the deer's ribcage as its breathing slowed. It twitched a final time and was still.

Jacob grinned up at Juniper, and she shuddered. She was frightened by the thing that looked like her father, horrified by what he had just done—but she was also curious.

"You killed it because a deer killed you, right?"

The hulder stood back up and looked down at the dead animal.

"But the one that killed you already died. And it was a buck, not a girl deer. I don't think this is right."

The Jacob hulder dropped the knife in the grass. It reached down and grabbed the deer's hind legs, then dragged her slowly away toward the barn. Juniper watched for a minute, unsure whether she ought to try to help or go wake Laura.

In the end, she did neither.

She ran. Away from the house, and the barn, and the thing that was not her father. She ran toward the distant bonfires.

• 23 •

Laura lay awake, listening to the wind outside, waiting for Juniper to return. Always a light sleeper, she had come awake with the feeling that the house was empty. She had never been able to sleep when her daughter was away.

The hoot of an owl sounded like a child crying, the whisper of the trees was a secret conversation. The old yellow farmhouse settled and groaned, and Laura stared at the ceiling.

At last she heard the front door open and quietly close again. She shut her eyes and laid very still, and eventually she heard the stairs creak, then footsteps along the hall. They stopped outside her room, and she heard heavy breathing on the other side of the door. The knob turned, and the door swung open. She cracked her eyes open just wide enough to see.

The dark shape in the doorway was not Juniper.

Laura sat up as the Jacob hulder took a step into the room. It stopped.

"What are you doing here?" Laura said. "What do you want?"

It took another step forward. She turned on the lamp next to her bed and the hulder held a hand up in front of its eyes, shielding them from the sudden light. It was bare chested and dirty, smeared with fresh blood, its hair matted. It lowered its hand and smiled at her and took off its pants.

"No," Laura said.

She spoke as if to a toddler, not willing to show it fear, but she thought of her mother and her pulse quickened. Anders had divulged too many details about Charlotte's final season on the farm, and about the Tor hulder she created. Charlotte had brought back a version of her husband from the earliest days of their marriage, and her relationship with it had not—according to Anders—been platonic.

But this was not Laura's version of Jacob; it was Juniper's creation. This Jacob was a decade younger, leaner and stronger, no gray in his beard and no stoop in his shoulders. They had both changed over the course of their marriage, and some of the initial passion had cooled, but she didn't miss that younger man anymore. She preferred to remember the mature husband and father he had become.

"No," Laura said again. She got up and grabbed Charlotte's robe from the end of the bed, wrapped it around herself and pointed to the bedroom door.

"Go outside," she said. "I don't want you here."

The hulder looked confused and hurt, and she felt a brief pang of pity. It turned and left, dragging its trousers behind it along the hall and down the stairs.

She waited until she heard the front door close, then ran down and locked it.

She turned on all the lights and searched the house to confirm she was alone. She grabbed the aebleskiver pan from the rack by the sink and swung it through the air a couple of times, testing it as a weapon, then went back upstairs and got dressed. She opened the bedroom window and leaned out. She could see the Jacob hulder near the tree line, moving in and out of shadows. It had dressed itself again, the black suit coat on backward so that a rectangle of its dirty white shirt was visible. She watched, and after a few minutes it plunged into the underbrush and disappeared.

A moth flew in and fluttered around before landing on

the wall, the big black spot on its wings a single eye staring down at her. She cursed at it and swung the heavy pan over her head, smashing it into the bedroom wall. Plaster crunched and fell in chunks at her feet; the poster of David Bowie tore loose and sagged to the floor. She realized she was shouting, and she backed away in surprise, lowering the pan. The moth circled her head once, found the open window, and flew out.

Laura forced herself to stand still and quiet until her breathing slowed. Her eyes stung, and she wiped them with the back of her hand. She contemplated the new hole in her bedroom wall and clenched her fist around the handle of the pan.

"Everything's wrong," she said. But her voice sounded flat to her, and far away.

She went back to bed and slipped under the duvet. She set the pan next to her, within easy reach, and returned to her lonely nighttime vigil.

• 24 •

THE DISTANT BONFIRES looked inviting, warm and bright, and Juniper thought it would feel nice to sit near one, maybe drink a beer, maybe accept a sweater or a blanket from some new Danish friend.

Watching the Jacob hulder butcher a deer in front of her had filled her with a mixture of emotions, and she felt an overwhelming need to get away from it and from the barn where her grandfather kept his scythes and sickles and long-handled knives.

She ran through the wheat, relishing the raspy feel of it against her skin. She had intended to find the hilltop and orient herself from there, but she got lost again and didn't stop running until she came out into the open behind a barn that matched her own, big and dull, a corrugated metal hangar.

She crept forward and around the side of the barn, curious about the low voices she heard on the other side. Three men were gathered on the flat plain in front of the byre, building a pile of kindling and hay and dead wood. One of the men had a plaster cast on his leg.

"Not gonna be easy," one of the men said.

"Never is," Anders Karlsen said.

"I meant," the first man said, "that this one is going to be especially hard."

Anders threw his armful of wood on the pile and shrugged.

The second man hefted a can and splashed the wood with sharp-smelling gasoline. When Anders turned to look out at the field Juniper slipped through the shadows and into the barn. This was not the friendly bonfire she had expected to find. This gathering of men seemed sad and furtive.

There were no animals in the barn, and no indication that there had ever been a horse or sheep or goat inside the tin structure. The people of Godhavn didn't seem to keep animals, and yet there were bales of hay stacked near the entrance.

Outside, someone lit the firewood, and there was a sudden flare of light through the open door. Juniper's eyes adjusted, and she could see the plain dirt floor; the walls around her were hung all around with the same sorts of implements she had seen in her grandfather's barn.

At the back of the big empty space was a giant birdcage. At least it looked like a birdcage, with thin wooden poles that were bent and curved and lashed together at the top. A heavy padlock held the door firmly shut.

Inside the cage was the little Magnus Karlsen hulder.

It reacted to the light, then to her, its single black eye bulging from its socket. Juniper smiled at it, and it smiled back. It had taken off its shirt, and its overalls hung loose at its waist, the straps dangling. It held out the limp furry thing in its hands for her to see: a rabbit, its pelt grimy with blood, entrails piled cold and sticky on the ground outside the bars of the cage.

Juniper reeled backward, and the Magnus hulder lost interest in her. It dropped the rabbit between its knees and began to scoop up handfuls of dirt, chaff, and dead brown leaves that had blown into the barn from outside, packing them furiously into the carcass.

The men's voices grew louder. They moved toward the barn, and Juniper looked around for a place to hide. Aside from the big cage, the bales of hay, and the hanging tools, the place was empty. If she hid behind the hay and the men came to add it to the fire, she would be caught. She grabbed the rung of a ladder and scampered up just as Anders entered the barn, leaning on one crutch.

Juniper laid down flat on the floor of the loft and peeked over the edge. She watched as Anders approached the cage below and produced a key from his pocket. He unfastened the padlock and swung the door open. The hulder stood and wiped its filthy hands on its bare chest, then ran them through its hair.

"It's time, buddy," Anders said. "You ready?"

He held out his hand and Magnus took it. The two of them walked slowly, hand in hand, out of the barn, their shadows stretching back behind them and fading away. The barn grew still and silent, the only sound a low murmur of voices outside and the faint crackling of the fire.

Below her, the rabbit twitched and got to its feet. It hopped once, twice, then keeled over.

Juniper held still and watched it for long minutes, but it didn't move again.

• 25 •

SHE HAD BEEN summoned to Godhavn five seasons in a
row and there was very little of Agnes Møller left, but
some small part of the hulder still felt affection for her sweet,
awkward employer Kaspar Henriksen. And yet, there were
things left undone, and no time for regrets.

In a foolishly dramatic gesture she had torn the skin from
Agnes's face, and so she waited until dark to carry Henriksen's
body through the alley, moving at a deliberate pace now that
the tentacled old things were warring for control of her limbs.

She paused by the seawall and sniffed the smoky air. There
were always so many bonfires this time of year, and the Agnes
hulder had been destroyed in four of them before. She looked
up and down the narrow walkway behind the shops and
buildings. The street ended at the hairdresser's, where Agnes
had kept a standing appointment for the third Wednesday of
the month for nearly a decade, back when she was alive. A few
yards beyond Heidi's Hair the pavement ended, and a gravel
road veered away from the sea toward open pastureland and
the tall silos of a granary mill in the distance. Everything was
dark and silent; no one stirred in Godhavn.

She laid Kaspar Henriksen's body on the wall. She pushed,
and Henriksen tumbled out of sight. Agnes hoisted herself
up and over and landed next to him in the packed dirt and
scrabbly weeds. A few feet away water lapped at the rocky

shore. The hulder took a moment to enjoy the cold spray, then got to work, opening Henriksen up and filling him full of grit, and dead brown plants, and dark, salty mud. She packed his cavities with debris, then filled his trouser pockets with smooth pebbles and shoved him out with the tide.

Agnes scrambled back up the bank and crawled over the seawall. She leaned against it for a long time, resting and weighing her options. She had torn a new gash in the Agnes skin along her left forearm and something was bulging out, black and pulsing to the steady rhythm of the water behind her. The air was cool, and Agnes closed her many eyes, enjoying the feel of the breeze on her faces.

Eventually she opened her eyes and pushed away from the wall. She would be found soon, she knew, probably as soon as the sun rose. She needed to find shelter, a place to hide and regroup, someplace cold where she could think.

Agnes would be visible from a mile away if she tried to burrow under the roots of the winter wheat across the bay. The short street ahead seemed to offer more possibilities. Heidi's Hair was useless, and so was Kaspar Henriksen's empty office. But next to the office, on the other side of the alley, was the bakery, and next to that, the cafe.

The hulder staggered toward the back door of the cafe. As she drew near, a thin tentacle slithered out from the wound in her arm and groped along the wall until it found the door-knob. It wrapped itself around the knob and pulled, and the door wrenched free, sagging to one side.

"We really ought to be more discreet," Agnes said aloud.

The tentacle slithered back beneath her skin and Agnes stepped over the twisted door into the cafe's kitchen. She did a quick mental inventory, making note of the espresso machine and coffee maker, two large ovens, a heavy-duty mixer, and the empty display cases that separated the kitchen from a small dining area. It was dark and silent, and the big glass window at the front of the shop looked out on an empty street.

The hulder tugged the door back into place. It wouldn't latch, so she fitted it into the jamb as well as she could, then moved to another door at the opposite end of the kitchen. This one was made of steel with a heavy lever that she pulled, releasing the catch to reveal a walk-in refrigerator filled with rolling racks of pastries and breads and cookies.

Agnes wheeled the racks out and wedged them between the chairs and tables on the other side of the counter. Then she packed two kringles, sticky with almond paste and custard, into the latch mechanism and eased herself onto the floor in the far corner of the refrigerator. The heavy door swung shut, the pastries mashed tight into the catch, preventing the lock from engaging and accidentally trapping her inside.

Cold settled over her skin, and she gradually began to feel stronger. She guessed she had maybe three or four hours before bakers would arrive to begin their morning preparations. By then she thought she ought to be strong enough.

She closed her eyes and fell into a deep sleep in which she dreamed of miniature people who screamed at her from a burned and empty landscape.

• 26 •

JUNIPER CLIMBED DOWN from the loft and crouched over the rabbit's remains. When it didn't move, she picked it up by its ears, turning it this way and that, examining it from different angles. Dust and sand sifted to the ground, but it was nothing more or less than a dead rabbit.

She dropped it and moved quietly to the barn door, peeking around the edge of the outside wall. Anders had led Magnus to the fire. The hulder's pale skin looked orange in the flickering light. Anders leaned down, his injured leg at an awkward angle in the plaster cast, and gave the thing that was his son a hug, then turned it around and flung it at the bonfire. The Magnus hulder stumbled over a crackling log and pitched face first into the flames.

Juniper gasped, but none of the three men standing at the fire's edge moved. They held rakes at their sides, and they stared as sparks twirled in the night air. Magnus stood up suddenly and began to shriek. Its howls of pain became a chorus of fury and desperation as its flesh cracked and thick tentacles snaked out, thrashing at the flames, groping for the men, who all stepped back out of its reach.

The tentacles multiplied and were joined by other dark shapes that erupted from the hulder's skin and folded back in on themselves. The Magnus Karlsen hulder grew, surging up and out like the black soda snakes Juniper had played with

every Fourth of July, sizzling and expanding well beyond the mass of a ten-year-old boy. It swelled and stretched, screeching and sputtering. And then it collapsed on itself, dissolving in a shower of sparks and ash, and it was gone.

A log shifted and the fire began to die out. At last, the men turned away, and Anders noticed Juniper standing in the wide opening of the barn door, frozen to the spot.

"Juniper?" he said.

She came to her senses and took a sideways step away from him.

"Juniper, come here."

"Hell no."

She turned and sprinted away from the barn, plunging into the winter wheat, her feet pounding the rutted dirt, her fists pumping as she zigzagged through the rows. She heard Anders calling to her as if from far away, and the other men giving chase, but they were moving slowly across the dark field.

She guessed at the direction of the yellow farmhouse and ran as fast as she could.

• 27 •

J UNIPER STILL wasn't home, and Laura was tired of waiting. She was putting off what clearly had to be done. She got up and slipped into her shoes and her jacket. She grabbed the pan from where it had fallen and left her room, crept down the stairs and outside. She didn't know where the Jacob hulder was. She held the handle of the pan in both hands, grateful for the weight of it, swinging it in narrow arcs as if stepping up to the plate.

The ground was covered with a thin layer of frost, but the farm was awake. Wind whistled in the nearby trees, crickets chirped in the grass, and bats squeaked under the eaves of the house. When she tuned out the ambient noise, she heard nothing big enough to be a person—or a hulder.

She scanned the field and the tree line.

"Jacob?"

She didn't expect an answer—the Jacob hulder didn't seem to be vocal—but her experience with hulders made her think it would respond in some way if it was nearby.

She stood at the edge of the trees and peered into the darkness. Nothing moved; nothing breathed. She turned and went to the barn where the big sliding doors stood open. Taking a deep breath, she stepped inside and cringed, waiting for the hulder to come rushing out at her. Again, there was nothing. She took another step and waited for her eyes to adjust to the moonlight, deciding the barn might be relatively safe for the moment. The hulder had already chosen the tools it wanted and, aside from its bizarre attempt at seduction, it had largely avoided enclosed spaces.

There was a power switch for the overhead lights, but she left it alone. The barn was only safe as long as the hulder didn't know she was there. It wouldn't help to advertise her location.

When she could see, she took stock of her surroundings. She was hoping to find a blowtorch or a propane tank, but there was none of that. As with every barn she had been in, there were rakes and shovels and loops of rope all neatly organized on hooks. Next to the rusty old car there was a big toolbox and a whip hanging on a nail. A whip wouldn't help her if the hulder attacked. A whip would only flay the skin from it and reveal the old things imprisoned beneath. In the far corner was a stack of hay bales. Five of them, each held together with twine. She smelled mildew, but the barn was watertight, the hay dry to the touch.

Tor Jessen had no animals to feed. Hulders did strange things to animals, and it was forbidden to raise them in Godhavn. But hay was flammable, and farmers always needed fuel for their end-of-season bonfires.

She grabbed the topmost bale and lifted, feeling its weight in her arms and back. She guessed it was close to a hundred pounds of old, dusty grass. She dropped it back on the pile and it bounced, landing at her feet. She bent again and got her hands under the twine and pulled it toward her, backing up to the door and pulling until she got it outside. She dragged it to the scorched spot in the grass and went back for the next one.

It took her half an hour to get them all outside the barn, arranged within the old circle of charred grass. After each bale she stopped and listened and heard nothing. When the fifth bale was in the circle, she sat on it and caught her breath. She watched the farm while her pulse rate slowed, waiting for the hulder or Juniper to appear, listening for anything that wasn't a bird or a squirrel. And then, finally, she heard something—"Mom!"

Laura sprang to her feet and scanned the field. Juniper was nowhere in sight.

"Mom!" Juniper's voice was farther away now.

"Junie!" Laura shouted.

"Mom?" Her voice was faint now, barely audible. Juniper was moving fast in the wrong direction. "Mom, they're chasing me!"

"Follow my voice, Junie! Can you hear me?"

There was no answer this time, and Laura kept calling her daughter's name, back and forth at the edge of the field. She was afraid she might get lost herself if she entered the tall rows of wheat and knew the wisest thing was to stay put and bring Juniper to her.

She shouted again, then forced herself to stand still and listen. She heard a rustling noise and for a moment felt hopeful that Juniper had found her way home—but realized a moment too late that the sound was behind her.

She turned, expecting to see the Jacob hulder. Something big brushed past her, sending her sprawling. She rolled over and looked up.

Moonlight shone through the antlers of a huge stag and created a halo effect at the edges of his short fur. He took a step toward her and she crawled away, then rolled sideways out of his path. When she sat up again she had a better vantage point and could see that it wasn't precisely a deer after all. Not anymore. Dead branches protruded from its hide, and when it moved she could hear twigs snapping under its coat. Dirt and leaves leaked from a deep gash in its belly. It moved like a puppet in a stop-motion movie, staggering and awkward, as if it had only just learned to walk.

It turned its head and its dark eyes glittered in the moonlight. Laura held herself still, hoping it might just wander away, but it made a chuffing sound deep in its chest and lunged at her, its legs tangled and clumsy but creating forward momentum, falling toward her. Laura couldn't get her arms up quickly enough. The deer's bulk was enough to crush her, its hooves sharp enough to tear her apart.

At the last possible moment, a dark shape charged out from the wheat and smacked into the deer's side, knocking it over. The ground shook beneath its body, raising a cloud of grit and chaff.

When the dust had settled the deer-thing lay still.

The Jacob hulder stood over it, the sleeves of its jacket torn off, and Tor's necktie wrapped tight around its throat. It carried the scythe, holding it loose at its side. It looked at her, and its eyes were black holes in its face. When it smiled at her Laura screamed.

It raised the scythe.

• 28 •

AGNES WOKE, feeling cold and refreshed. She tried to stand and her right leg split open, spilling a gelatinous black mess out over the walk-in's floor. The hulder concentrated and reeled the goop back in, but her skin had become so thin it was nearly transparent.

The hulder was calculating its next move when the heavy door swung open. An old woman stood on the other side holding a shotgun, the barrel resting on her forearm, aimed at Agnes's center mass. A canvas bag was slung over her shoulder.

"We know you," the hulder said. Its voices echoed off the thick steel walls. "You're the nosy old woman who lives by the water and drives the red truck. We've seen you at Heidi's."

"My name is Anna Schmidt," the woman said, "and I know who you are, too. You used to be Agnes Møller. We had a friend in common. Kaspar Henriksen?"

"Kaspar Henriksen is gone," the hulder said.

"I know," Anna said. "He visited me this evening. I should say what was left of him visited me. He was soaking wet and packed with dirt and rocks. You did that to him?"

"We don't understand." A thin tendril oozed from its spine to the floor and inched along the baseboard, spinning out from it like a fishing line. "You make things like us that last a season, but the things *we* make fail within minutes. It makes no sense to us."

"I've wondered the same thing," Anna said. "It took me a while, but I think I figured it out." She waved the barrel of the shotgun. "You should stop doing that with the tentacle. I'm not going to let you flank me."

The tendril withdrew into Agnes's skin.

"That won't work on us," the hulder said. "The gun. It will hurt, but it will not stop us."

"I know," Anna said. "But it makes me feel better to have it."

"If you step aside, we will leave."

"Maybe I would if I'd only brought the gun," Anna said. "But I planned ahead."

She set the shotgun behind her on a rack of day-old rye bread. She reached into her canvas bag and pulled out a propane torch, bright yellow with a red ignition switch.

"*Medbring det rigtige værktøj til det rigtige job*," Anna said. "That's something that sweet, silly Kaspar used to say."

She pressed the trigger, and a bright blue flame sparked to life at the end of the torch's barrel. The Agnes hulder shrank back against the wall and Anna gave it a pitying look.

"Let's get this over with," she said. "I've got another appointment."

• 29 •

JUNIPER HEARD Laura scream and stopped where she was, breathing hard, trying to listen. She could hear thrashing sounds somewhere behind her, one of the men chasing her through the wheat. And—even farther off, in the direction of Godhavn—she saw a plume of smoke rising up, gray against the white moon. Her mother screamed again. Juniper turned toward the sound and ran.

Minutes later she came out of the wheat onto the wide expanse of land the hulder had harvested. She could see the barn ahead and she sprinted for it.

The Jacob hulder lumbered into her line of sight, using its tall scythe as a walking stick, a fistful of Laura's hair in his other hand. Laura was fighting it, kicking and shouting as the hulder dragged her across the driveway toward the gaping black maw of the barn door.

"Dad!"

The hulder turned toward her, smiling, its eyes black and empty. Juniper could hardly breathe, but she kept running.

"Let Mom go!"

The hulder seemed momentarily confused. It loosened its grip on Laura's hair and she pulled herself free, rolling and scrambling across the gravel toward Juniper. They met at the edge of the field and collapsed into each other's arms, both of them gasping for breath.

The hulder watched them, grinning, moving the scythe slowly back and forth as if trying to decide what to do with it. There was a deer lying on its side in the grass, leaves and dead branches protruding from it at random angles. When she had calmed down enough to speak, Juniper pulled away from her mother.

"I saw," she said. "I saw what we have to do."

Laura shook her head, but Juniper went on. "They burned Magnus. His dad did. Magnus was made out of weird creatures. The tentacles that came through the hole in my closet—that's what's inside them." She thought of the carvings on her grandmother's box. "We have to burn it, don't we?"

"It's part of the ritual," Laura said. "What I was trying to tell you. They have to be burned at the end of the season."

"And it's the end of the season?"

"I didn't think it was time yet," Laura said. "The crops aren't in."

"Your friend Anders said something about a shorter season, or maybe a smaller crop."

The Jacob hulder had become impatient and was moving toward them now, the scythe swinging in purposeful arcs ahead of it.

"You have to end it," Juniper said.

"*You're* supposed to do it. You created him. It's your responsibility."

"I can't."

The hulder was picking up speed, marching steadily toward them. Laura grabbed Juniper and pulled her around the side of the barn. They leaned against the dull tin arc of the building, and Laura reached into her pocket, pulled out a book of matches.

She pressed them into Juniper's hand.

"I'll distract him," she said. "There's bales of hay out there.

I was going to try to lure it into the circle. The hay's pretty dry, so if you just get the edges . . . maybe hit more than one spot around the outside of it."

"And then what?"

"I'll help when it's time. Just try to get a fire going."

Before Juniper could object Laura was gone, running around the back of the barn. A moment later she reappeared, racing across the grass toward the house. Juniper stepped out from the shelter of the barn's shadow and nearly ran into the Jacob hulder. It was watching Laura, and Juniper drew back before it could see her. It tore off its necktie and threw it on the ground, then grabbed the scythe with both hands and chased after Laura. Juniper counted to ten, then followed.

The bales of hay were arranged in a clumsy semicircle not far from the barn. Juniper kept watching for the hulder, worried it might pop up behind her, but it was intent on catching Laura, who had reversed direction and was weaving back and forth at the edge of the field, fading back and springing out to confuse the thing.

Juniper pulled out a match and tried to light it. Too slow; it didn't spark. She tried again, but her hands were shaking, and she dropped the box of matches. She glanced up and didn't see her mother or the hulder.

"What's taking so long?"

Laura was suddenly there, having circled the house and come up behind Juniper. She was carrying a kitchen knife and a dirty rolled-up dishcloth. "We need fire," she said.

"I'm too nervous," Juniper said.

"Get back!"

The hulder rounded the corner of the house and charged across the yard. It lunged at them, tripping over a bale and into the circle of scorched grass. The scythe was under it and it fell on the long blade—the tool plunged through it, the tip pushing up through its back. It rolled over and there was a ripping sound as pulsing black tentacles burst out across the ground. The hulder grunted and wrenched the scythe from its body, tossing it to the side. It crawled to one of the bales and pulled itself to its feet, then twitched as the masses of black stuff were drawn back into it. It was not quite human-shaped anymore; it bulged strangely and its quivering limbs were much too long, like an orangutan wearing human skin. But it took an awkward step forward, then another.

"The matches," Laura said. "Where are they?"

Juniper pointed, and Laura felt around on the ground until she found them. She lit one and pushed the tiny flame at the nearest bale. She moved the match back and forth, and a few pieces of hay smoldered, then fizzled out. She lit another and held it against a corner of the dishtowel. It smoldered, and she draped it over the end of a bale. The hulder stumbled toward them as a thin tendril of smoke rose from the hay. Then it was out of the circle, moving fast.

"Go that way," Laura said.

She shoved Juniper and scrambled away in the other direction, blindly lighting and throwing matches into the hay. Juniper stayed near the hay, hoping the hulder would follow her and give her mother time to start the fire, but it didn't. It turned its back to her and followed Laura, moving faster and faster, helped by tentacles that snaked out and pulled it along.

"Over here!" Juniper shouted.

She waved her arms, and the hulder half turned, distracted. Its left foot turned under it and the ankle snapped, but the hulder kept moving around the circle, black goo mushing against the ground under the useless foot.

Stray pieces of straw glowed along the edges of the bales in her mother's wake, and then a section of the hay burst into flames, the fire spreading quickly from one bale to another. The hulder shrieked and recoiled, and Laura jumped to her feet. She ran at it, brandishing her knife, but it lashed out and knocked her down. Her head hit the ground hard, the knife flew from her hand, and she didn't get up.

"Mom!"

The hulder turned, smiling, and held out its arms to Juniper.

"You're *not my dad*!" She stood rooted to the ground, unable to move as it advanced on her, wearing her father's face.

"I wish you would go away!" she said. "I hate you!"

It stopped moving and lowered its arms. In the flickering firelight its eyes were moist and confused, and Juniper felt a twinge of pity for it. She took a step forward.

A gunshot shattered the spell and sent the hulder staggering sideways, black ichor bubbling down its cheek. With a burst of adrenaline Juniper ran at it. She put her arms out and shoved, and the hulder toppled backward into the blackened circle, brushing against a hay bale as it fell. The bale tipped over in a fountain of sparks and tumbled over its leg. The hulder roared as its trousers caught fire, and it stood, but the flames hemmed it in now, the blaze jumping from bale to bale. The Jacob hulder stood in place and watched as the fire advanced. It smiled again at Juniper, then seemed to multiply and fold in on itself again and again, voices mumbling and screaming and arguing in different languages.

Juniper backed away from the fire and went to her mother. Laura's pulse was strong and steady, and when Juniper stroked her cheek she opened her eyes.

"Are you okay?"

"I don't know," Juniper said. "There's somebody else out here."

Laura sat up and they both peered out into the darkness, their eyes struggling to adjust to the night beyond the bright flames. At last Juniper was able to pick out the dark figure of a man standing on the other side of the circle. He leaned awkwardly on a crutch and raised a hunting rifle at her.

"I told you I'd help out around here," Anders Karlsen said.

• 30 •

Juniper stepped to her left, and Anders mirrored her, pushing forward with his crutch to keep his balance. Between them, the dying fire crackled and spat, hemmed in by smoldering hay bales. A dark smudge on the ground was all that remained of the Jacob hulder.

"Stay where you are," Anders said. "Both of you."

"Please leave, Anders," Laura said. "It's over now."

"Go home, Farmer Bob," Juniper said. "My mom's not interested."

"I said it's over," Laura said again.

"You know that's not true," Anders said.

He limped around the outside of the smoldering circle. The rifle wavered in the crook of his elbow, its barrel pointing away in every direction.

"You *have to* end her!" he said.

Laura scrambled across the fire on all fours, trying to get to the other side and stop Anders. She was moving too fast to feel the heat, but her right knee came down hard on the handle of the scythe, and a bolt of pain shot up through her hip. She bit her lip to keep from crying out and waved her hand at Anders, hoping to draw his attention so Juniper could escape back into the fields.

"She's different," Laura said. She tried to stand but her

leg gave out, and she sagged against a smoking hay bale. "She wasn't made here. She's not tied to your harvest."

"You're not thinking straight, Laura," Anders said. "I understand. I lost my family too." He hadn't stopped moving, closing the distance between himself and Juniper, who stood rooted to the ground, listening to them.

"She doesn't know," Laura said.

"Mom?" Juniper said.

Laura ignored her. She kept her eyes on Anders and his rifle. "She's not like the others," she said. "She made another hulder. They're not supposed to be able to do that."

"It was a second-generation hulder that lasted all of two days." But she had his attention now. He had stopped hobbling toward her daughter and was half-turned, squinting in the direction of her voice. She realized he couldn't see her among the blackened shapes of the bales.

"It wasn't perfect," she said. "But have you ever seen that before? I know you haven't."

"What are you guys talking about?" Juniper said.

"Just go, Junie. Go in the house."

"I'm dreaming again," Juniper said. Her voice was barely audible over the chirps of insects in the wheat. "My dreams have been weird lately."

"What was your tribute, Laura?" Anders said. "What was the offering from the field?"

"Grass." Laura felt around her on the ground and found the scythe. Using it as a crutch, she got to her feet, careful to keep her weight off her injured leg. "Just some grass from our backyard," she said. She shuffled toward Anders and around him, and he swiveled in place, keeping her in sight. "I remembered the ritual and I used what I had."

"How do you know your yard isn't turning brown and dying right now back in America? As soon as that happens, she's going to kill you, Laura."

"It's grass," Laura said. "Grass lasts forever."

She was between Anders and Juniper now, with the field behind them and the remains of the fire at Anders's back.

"Grass is perennial," Anders said. "It has a one-year cycle. How far along was it when you made your hulder?"

"But I'm not—wait, I," Juniper said, "I'm not like Dad. I know who I am. I mean, I'm totally the same as always."

Laura shook her head and looked away.

"Aren't I?" Juniper said.

Anders limped forward again, edging closer to them. "This is for your own good, Laura Loaf," he said.

"I haven't been Laura Loaf in years," Laura said, "and you don't get to decide what's good for me."

She brought the scythe up like a baseball bat and swung wildly, hitting him in the throat with its shaft. Anders stumbled and coughed, then pivoted on his good leg and grabbed the scythe. He used it to pull Laura closer, then dropped it and slapped her across the face. She fell and Anders bent over her, raising his hand again.

"Don't hit my mom," Juniper said. Her voice was low, but confident. There was a second voice that echoed her words and reverberated beneath them. She took a step forward and raised her hand. "This is a very weird night for me, and you're not helping at all," she said.

"Juniper, no," Laura said. "Don't hurt him."

"My name is Juniper Roux. I live in Blue Valley with my mom, and I want to go home now."

"We can go back," Laura said. "We can leave here if you want and go back home."

Juniper shook her head and kept moving toward Anders, more quickly than he could back up. His cast thumped on the ground, and he fumbled with the rifle, trying to keep his balance and aim it.

"I'm a person," Juniper said. "Why would you say I'm not

even a person? You just think everything's weird because this place is weird. Take back what you said. Both of you, take it back right now!"

She lunged forward, and Anders tripped, scrambling backward, dragging the rifle, until he was stopped by the smoldering remains of a hay bale. In one smooth motion, he raised the rifle and steadied it. He fired, and Juniper screamed. She was jolted off her feet, flopped to the ground, and lay motionless.

• 31 •

LAURA GRABBED the scythe and pulled herself up. Her face stung where Anders had slapped her, and her leg throbbed with pain.

"Junie?"

Juniper laid still and silent, a dark shape against the swaying crops.

"We still have to burn it," Anders said.

Laura ignored him and took a step toward her daughter, but stopped when she saw Juniper's arm twitch. Juniper rolled over and stood up, facing the dark fields, her head cocked to one side as if she was listening to something Laura couldn't hear. Laura called her name again and Juniper turned, her face expressionless. Her overalls were torn, and a gaping hole was visible in her chest. Tentacled things writhed in the formless void contained by her skin.

"Mom?"

Laura leaned on the scythe and hobbled across the grass to her daughter. She took off her jacket and draped it over Juniper's shoulders, pulling it closed over the void and fastening the top few buttons as quickly as she could, her fingers trembling.

"It was the accident, wasn't it?" Juniper said. Her obsidian eyes glinting in the firelight. "The deer didn't just kill Dad, did it? I'm like him. A weird thing."

"You're not like him," Laura said.

She could hear Anders approaching, and she pushed Juniper behind her. She turned so she could see Anders, but she kept herself between them, still blocking Anders's way forward with her body. In her hurry to cover Juniper up, she had dropped the scythe, and now she eyed it nervously, weighing the time it would take to pick it up against Anders's ability to fire another shot. He was moving slowly, dragging his broken leg, the rifle held loose at his side. He stopped several yards from them and held out one hand in a calming gesture.

"Look, I got carried away," he said. "This has been rough for all of us, Laura, but I shouldn't have hit you."

"Just go," Laura said.

"Help me rebuild the fire," he said. "Later we can talk."

Juniper bent and picked up the scythe. She stood back up, holding it casually across her body with both hands.

"Go to the house, Mom," she said. Her voice was almost unrecognizable. "I think I know how to use this thing."

"Laura, you've got to listen to reason," Anders said.

"I'm not going to let you burn me, Mr. Karlsen," Juniper said. "I don't think my mom wants that either."

Juniper brushed past Laura and swept the scythe through the air. Anders hopped sideways and lost his grip on the rifle. He grimaced and hobbled back toward the dying fire.

"You're pretty fast for a cripple," Juniper said. She chuckled, the sound deep and watery.

"Junie, please don't," Laura said.

"I told you to go inside, Mom. I'll be along in a while."

"She'll kill us both," Anders said.

"We get it, man," Juniper said. "I'm a monster."

"Laura, she will most definitely kill you," Anders said. "She's already turning. Think about what happened to your mother."

Juniper stopped moving and gazed at Laura, the scythe

brushing against the brown grass at her feet, her head cocked to one side again.

Laura remembered Jacob's beard with its flecks of gray, and his middle-age paunch, and she thought of her mother's empty cupboards and unused spice rack. The fire had become a faint glow, reflected by the corrugated walls of the barn in a way that reminded her of colorful fish. She saw the same golden hue rolling across the wheat in the field and realized the sun was rising.

Laura looked at Anders and shrugged. "At least my mother wasn't alone," she said.

She turned and walked away, up the driveway and across the yard. She almost laughed when she saw the aebleskiver pan lying in the grass where she had dropped it. She picked it up, brushed it off, and carried it to the kitchen door.

She didn't look back when Anders started screaming.

EPILOGUE

L AURA MIXED the ingredients in the same big bowl and
used the same plastic spatula to spoon batter into the
pan. She added a little strawberry jam, not too much this
time, and was gratified when it didn't ooze out of the cakes.

She cast an eye at her mother's cupboard where the
unopened box of rat poison sat waiting. It would be easy to
sprinkle some of the poison on the aebleskiver, like powdered
sugar.

Not just easy, it would be the right thing to do. Just to
give herself an edge.

But she didn't.

She looked up when the kitchen door banged open.
Juniper rested the scythe against the wall in the corner and
went to the little round table. She pulled out a chair and sat
and watched Laura flip the round cakes in their pan.

Tires crunched on the gravel driveway outside, and Laura
filled the coffeemaker with water. She scooped coffee into the
basket and got an extra mug from the cupboard. She opened
the box of poison, poured it into a sugar bowl, and set it
in the middle of the table. Then she sat down across from
the monster who looked like her daughter and waited, listening for footsteps on the threshold, watching the yellow light
through the homemade curtains, and enjoying the moment.

Because the moment was everything.

ACKNOWLEDGMENTS

Thank you to Andrea Mutti, who believed in this story and made such pretty pictures.

And to Riley Rossmo, for inspiring me.

I am deeply grateful to Palle Schmidt for his expertise in all things Danish, and to Seth Peck for his expertise in all things Lovecraftian.

I am also indebted to Seth Fishman and everyone at the Gernert Company, and to Tze Chun, Sebastian Girner, Amy Sumerton, and the crew at TKO.

And, of course, to my wife and son, without whom the rest wouldn't matter.

—Alex

Special thanks to my wife, Rachel, and my sons, Alvise and Giacomo.

—Andrea

ABOUT THE AUTHOR

ALEX GRECIAN is the *New York Times* bestselling author of *The Yard* and its four sequels, as well as the contemporary thriller *The Saint of Wolves and Butchers*, the ebook *The Blue Girl*, and scads of short stories. He is the writer and co-creator of two comic book series: *Rasputin* and *Proof*, both for Image Comics. Both series are currently being developed for TV. His books have been translated into numerous languages and are available around the world. He lives in the American Midwest with his wife and son.

alexgrecian.com
@alexgrecian

ABOUT THE ILLUSTRATOR

ANDREA MUTTI is a comic book artist who started his career illustrating superhero comics in his native country, Italy. He has worked on a wide range of detective titles for various French publishers. He has also worked with Marvel, DC, Vertigo, Dark Horse, Top Cow, IDW, BOOM! Studios, Adaptive, Dynamite, Stela, Titan, and Vault.

andrearedmutti.com.

VISIT TKO PRESENTS.COM

Get behind-the-scenes content,

including early drafts, notes,

and inspirations from the

writer and illustrator.

TKOPRESENTS.COM
ONEEYEOPEN-BONUS

PICK UP THE OTHER TITLES IN OUR FIRST WAVE OF ILLUSTRATED NOVELLAS!

Brood X

By Joshua Dysart
Illustrated by M.K. Perker

With the Red Scare on the rise and a looming fear of nuclear war gripping the nation, seven laborers gather under the smoldering heat of an Indiana summer to begin a curious project: constructing a bomb shelter . . . in the middle of nowhere. But when the emergence of a once-in-a-century cicada swarm ushers in a series of increasingly unlikely accidents on the site, the survivors start eying one another with more than just suspicion.

A nail-biting murder mystery about the horrors that divide us all. It will leave you guessing until the very last page. By bestselling author Joshua Dysart with illustrations by internationally-renowned artist M.K. Perker.

$9.99

Blood Like Garnets

By Leigh Harlen
Illustrated by Maria Nguyen

A modern-day witch can knit the
dead back to life for a fearsome
price. Follow a lone predator's
surprising night on a bloody hunt.
Join a carefree karaoke night with
friends that ends in blood, tears, and dark revelations.

Beneath the placid surface of family, love, and reason, the
line between monster and human blurs, love becomes
obsession, and voices long silenced demand to be heard in
Leigh Harlen's blood-curdling debut.

Dive into the terrors that lurk behind every corner and
in every shadow with these flesh-crawling tales. Contains
eight spine-tingling horror stories by Leigh Harlen with
illustrations by Maria Nguyen.

$9.99